A Distant Neighbor

A Distant Neighbor

This book is a work of fiction. Any names, characters, places, or incidents are products of author's imagination and are fictitious or used in ficticious manner. Any resemblance or similarity to actual people, places, events, or establishments is purely coincidental .

This book is for ages 18+ due to some sexual content.

Playlist

BlameIt on the Rain - He Is We
Until the Credits Roll - Ben Dunnill
Stay A Little Longer - NoThingz
Empty Room - Jamie Miller
New Brain - Naomi Scott
Skinny Dipping - Sabrina Carpenter
November - McKenna Grace

Glimpse of Us -Joji

Prologue

"When there's rainfall, I fall. Let me explain. I'll fall into a state of panic. I'll fall into a state of anxiety. I'll fall into a state of dread. I mentally prepare myself for something unfortunate to take place.

"All my young life I've associated such depressing weather with tragedy. The tragedy of having witnessed a car wreck where a young life was taken. The misfortune of having to bury my pet rabbit in the rain because it lasted for days and my poor little Sugar's body could no longer stay above ground. The horror of getting caught in the rain with classmates at school and a boy slipped as he ran for cover and bashed his face on the concrete. I watched his blood pool in the rapidly growing puddles. I had never seen so much blood before then. It scared me.

"Then of course, having watched my mother grow sicker and sicker from what she told me was a thing called pneumonia and explained to me how she caught it. She only had it for a few days but she went through a terrible time. I vowed never to catch that sickness.

"Well into middle school I had grown anxiety around rainy weather and for those reasons, I could never understand the coziness of a stormy day. It didn't help that I got made fun of for it. And that didn't help to keep me from being a target for kids. It was quite awful. I hated it."

"Do you still hate it? Even now?"

"No, because now, when there's rainfall, I fall in a different way these days. I fall more and more in love with you. Now, I love the rain. It's how I see you."

His mouth curls slightly upward. "I was hoping you'd say that."

part one

CHAPTER 1

November

At the sound of thunder I know it's time to go home. Normally, it would be enough that the air feels like rain is on the way for me to skip out on a run but I couldn't help but to start my day off strong, filled with energy and motivation, and running is always a convenient way to do that.

The sun soaks energy into my brown skin and breathing the fresh air into my lungs continues to cleanse the negative remnants of my last disaster of a relationship that was Miles, which is much needed if I'm to passionately create covers for clients, burn off last night's Chinese takeout, and get over the stupid breakup.

Sure, a breakup that ended a year ago, but the pain of being used still lingers. The betrayal continues to haunt me. When a man even looks my way I'll look back and wonder if he is an honest partner or a fucking loser. That seems to be my radar for knowing if I might be ready to get back into the dating scene or not. I obviously have to tell Liv that I most definitely am not so that she can stop trying to set me up.

Running also resets my brain from loss of sleep from an endless misery, but I can't complete my run if it's going to rain, and the fresh air reeks of it close by. The humid air and muggy stench churns my stomach and throws off my momentum. I've never been the type to play in the rain, splash in puddles, or call it cozy. It is, in fact, the very opposite to me. I quite find it annoying with how loud it can get when it pours. It ruins my makeup, makes me cold, not to mention bad luck, and, oh! Can't forget, it feels traumatic to me.

Many have called me weird for it, if you can believe it. I've learned that I possess that unpopular opinion and I'm perfectly content with that. My best friend, Liv, is one of those many who loves it when it rains and ever since we were girls in high school, she's made it her life's mission to convert me. She knows that I see it as a shower of bad luck, so she tries to make it so that I can associate it with comfort the way she does, which is why she's bringing breakfast in a bit.

I've never admitted this to her but I've come to associate it with her. Rain means we get to hang out, and for that, I have become only somewhat indifferent to the nasty weather.

As I run closer to my house I take out my earbuds and stuff them into the pocket of my shorts when I see Helena, my neighbor, waving me down. Now, although my parents had strongly encouraged their shy and apprehensive daughter to move into the safe and quaint neighborhood of Everglow of Hopeheart Town, I am of the sort who is at her most okayest when I keep to myself. The sweet old woman often tries to create a neighborly relationship with me but I simply don't have the interest in having neighborly relations with anyone. I would prefer to stay invisible.

Nevertheless, I am no asshole, so I mentally prepare for a friendly banter. *Hi, how are you? Looks like it's going to be a wet one today, huh?* And then keep walking, don't stop. *Alright, well, I'll leave you to your gardening. Stay dry!* Yeah. That's a good one.

She looks up from her garden and that would be my cue to play the friendly neighbor before she does, but she comes at me with a speed that I'm not used to seeing from her. "November!"

"Hey, Helena! How are you?"

"November, women shouldn't be running in their bras, dear," she scolds.

She goes off script but I'll continue what I rehearsed. "Looks like it's going to be a wet one today, huh?" I laugh, ignoring her unsolicited suggestion of my workout attire.

"You're much too exposed. You'll catch a cold. And men could be, you know," she glances at my chest, "staring."

I nod, still slowly slinking to my door, not wanting to stand around with her carrying on with a conversation that may turn unpleasant if I let her continue to judge me. I awkwardly add, "Alright, well, I'll leave you to your gardening. Stay dry!"

"Not all men are gentlemen, November! That's all!" she shouts, loud enough for the whole of Everglow to hear.

I panic, unsure how to respond, then laugh and wave before closing the door. I take a peek out of the peephole to see how long she will stand there. She looks around to see if anyone has witnessed our interaction, then somberly treks back to her yard, watering her perfectly blossomed spring flowers, despite the rain that's coming.

Sometimes I feel bad for avoiding having a conversation with her. I just don't know how to be comfortable with people who are so blunt they border on rude. She's not a cranky old hag or anything evil like that, but she's not exactly easygoing to my standards either. Give me someone awkward or shy or klutzy or odd, and then maybe I could have some confidence to be who I am.

I clamour about in my kitchen for a large glass of water. I take a seat on the sofa, gulping every last drop and browse through my socials on my phone while I catch my breath.

I'm tagged on Instagram. Liv posted and tagged me in a photo she took of herself with Eren and a couple other people she is sort of friends with—Tessa and Levi. They're all smiling for her photo, each one holding up a mimosa at a local diner. She captioned it *The gang's (almost) all here!*

I'm tagged in another photo, this time by Eren. It's a selfie of his face lazily resting on a fist looking bored. He captioned it *Bored.* My face warms. I keep myself from smiling even though there's no one here to hide it from. I heart both photos and jump in the shower. Yes, a real shower, one not riddled with bad luck, only pure ecstasy.

When I'm out of the shower I make myself a hot cup of coffee. I baby the hot beverage as I work on a commissioned book cover until I hear a knock on the door twenty minutes later.

I open it to Liv holding up a brown paper bag. "I got your favorite," she sing-songs cheerfully. "I study her, wondering what the uppity mood is about. Without breaking her smile, she speaks without moving her mouth. "You better let me in because your neighbor won't stop staring at me," she also sing-songs, side-eyeing in Helena's direction.

I poke my head out and our eyes meet.

"No! Don't...ugh." Liv shut her eyes, not wanting to be in the crossfire of the stare-off.

I wave so that she knows that I am aware that she is not minding her own business.

"Now, why would you do that, Em? That was so freaking awkward."

I step aside so that she can enter. "I got to let her know that I see her looking too closely at my business. Earlier, she was on my ass about running in a sports bra because men can't control themselves."

"Oh, god," she spits. She brings my food to me on the sofa as I finish adding sparkle to a sword to the art piece on my Ipad. "Ooh, that looks fucking amazing. Nice work, as usual."

I put my Ipad and pen down on the coffee table and accept the plate from her. A veggie omelet and a side of hash. "And you? Are you almost done?" I'm referring to the book's formatting. That's what she does in our fast-growing business.

"I guess I should work on that today, seeing as how you're almost finished."

I take a bite and groan with satisfaction. "My god, I love that place. Thanks for feeding me."

"I almost didn't. I wish you would have just met us there."

With a mouth full of food, because I am not above speaking with a mouth full of food, I say, "But it was fine because I saw that you ran into your other best friends."

The thick sarcasm isn't lost on her and her eyes roll away from me. "They're just people Eren and I used to work with."

"Well, they can all be your new best friends. I'm sure they're not trying to work their way out of the trenches of a bad breakup."

"Oh, not this again." Liv covers her face with a pillow. "Please, enough with the self-depricating. He's not even worth this much heartache. You know that. The guy was a tool and a mooch and a loser." She removes the pillow, revealing a big smile. "But you know who is not a loser? Eren." Her smile stretches wider like the Cheshire Cat. "He was hoping to see you this morning. And no, I definitely did not miss that photo he tagged you in. Rude as hell, if you ask me. Tessa, Levi, and I were perfectly good company, thank you very much. He was the one being a sour puss because his favorite person wasn't there."

I throw my plate away, pour us some coffee, and sit back on the sofa without responding to what she said.

"I mean, I don't think it needs to be a relationship if you're not ready. I think he would be perfectly fine keeping things casual. I thought that's what you were wanting?"

That's exactly what I told her I wanted but only to get her off my ass about moving on. "Oh my god, Liv, tell me you all didn't talk about this at breakfast. Tell me this wasn't supposed to be some sort of plan to hook us up."

Liv scoffs. "Oh, don't be ridiculous. He's too obviously infatuated with you that he literally doesn't need to say a single word. Like, come on, you're not that dense. I know you've been pickin' up what he's been puttin' down, but what you don't see is the way he lights up whenever you come around and the way he pays closer attention to a conversation whenever your name is mentioned. It's been a year of this and, frankly, it's beginning to be painful to watch."

I would be lying if I said that I don't notice his come-ons. However, I don't know if he makes it obvious on purpose or if he just can't help himself. He's never actually asked me out on a date. Either way, I smirk thinking about it.

"Aha! So you *are* aware! And what, are you that uninterested? Do you not find him attractive? Honestly, and you know this, if I wasn't seeing someone when I first met him on my first day at that stupid restaurant I would have been all over him. But then he met you and now it's far too late for me since he is all about you. At this point, it would be weird if I even tried to pursue him. So really, you can't pass him up. I can't let you. It'll be a waste. One of us has to snag him before someone else does and it can't be me."

"Liv, I think you need another boyfriend to put all of this...pent up energy into," I tease.

She flings herself back into the sofa, covering her face with a pillow again. "Ugh, I know! I really thought he was the one."

"Please tell me that's a joke."

"I mean, I hoped he would be the one. Ugh, why did he have to be such an asshole? He was so cute."

"Oh sure, that controlling behavior was super cute, alright."

"Yes, yes, I get it. Moving on. I have a question. When I do end up meeting someone would you go on a double date with me? With Eren? It doesn't have to be an official date, just a double date for funsies."

I imagine what that could look like. Eren is great. He's cute, kind, funny. My pause is not because of him at all but rather looking at it from my last relationship not long after I moved into this house. Miles had used me to live here free of rent with the false intention of finding a job. He gave me just enough to say that he cared about me and our relationship until I eventually caught on to his true motive—to mooch.

I didn't even have much for him to mooch off of in the

first place. I was working as a housekeeper at a hotel near Liv's restaurant when we launched our website and officially started our business. It was only when we weren't going to have enough time to work our other jobs when we finally quit and began fully working for ourselves. Miles saw the potential flow of money that was about to come in and figured he could be taken care of, and that wasn't the kind of person I wanted as a partner.

He became dead weight. An anchor to my creativity for the work I needed to do. For the work I always dreamed of doing. And now that I have established myself financially, I honestly haven't a single desire to expect anything from a man. I'm content with my work and good with not having to worry about a man's feelings. A weak man who would gaslight his woman to think that she's not doing enough for him until all she can think about is all that he wants, forgetting herself in the scramble to make things right. I don't feel like risking going back to that just to be able to say that I have a boyfriend. That I am in a "committed" relationship. The label means nothing to me now.

Though, would I go on a "date" with Eren just for funsies? I suppose, as long as I make it clear to him that commitment will not be on the table. "Liv, I'll make you a deal. If you find a *good* man—someone with some class for once—then I will definitely go on a double date with you."

"You're not just saying that because you don't think I could actually get a classy man, are you?" She raises a suspicious brow.

She is crazy if she believes that I don't believe that she could land a man with class. She is drop dead gorgeous. Her shiny jet black hair gives her a dark and edgy vibe. Her finger tattoos give her a cool edginess that a lot of men seem to be drawn to. Her natural tanned complexion always makes her look like she just got back from vacationing. She's smart and talented. She's the whole damn package, yet sometimes it's like she doesn't realize her own worth and ends up settling with men beneath her. Although I've been told that that's where she likes her men, literally.

"You could, easily, you just don't choose them. Because you're stupid. You're a stupid girl when it comes to picking flowers out of the weeds and one of these days, those weeds will come with thorns and poke holes in your heart."

"Weeds don't have thorns, dumbass."

"Yes, they could have, stupid. They especially do in my metaphor."

Liv chucks a pillow at me.

Thunder booms and we both jump. Aggressive pouring rain follows soon after.

Liv grabs a throw blanket from the chair beside her and makes herself comfortable, stretching her legs out onto my lap as she turns on the TV. "Hopefully, with all this rain, I'll see some nice blooms."

"If it doesn't drown them first."

"Hush it and tune in to the static of the downpour. Let it ease all that gross hostility you harbor."

I snort. "Static puts you at ease?"

"Shut up and get cozy, Em."

"If we were in my ideal cozy place you wouldn't have to wait for the flowers to bloom."

"And what is your ideal cozy place?"

"A sunny sky over a grassy knoll. Filled with flowers. Populated with butterflies—not men. And no rain."

CHAPTER 2

Declan

I AWAKE TO THE SOUND OF THE USUAL BIRDSONGS. I WOULD FIND IT soothing if they weren't practically screaming their songs, though. However, their attempts can be somewhat entertaining, just preferably not first thing in the morning. Maybe one day they'll improve and I'll wake up feeling like a Disney princess. "Keep at it, birds," I say at the window. "You'll get it someday."

I turn on the coffee maker and get ready for another day at the studio, where people who come and go often either look like they are about to walk in New York Fashion Week or like they walked out of a JC Penny catalog. Although we do business with a lot of interesting people, life has become mundane, and I ponder this notion while the coffee drips into the pot, in the silence of my house, my life. That's what my life has become, at the sweet age of twenty-five. Stagnant, comfortable, predictable.

Wake up, talk to the birds, have coffee, go to work, come home, drink beer, repeat. Sometimes I'll hang out with Dean and Karina on the weekends, but when I'm not, I feel like I've come to the end of a road. I got the career I shot for and it's been great. It's been great for the last five years. Now what?

The birds continue to sing in the tree outside my house. I put my slippers on and meet them outside. I bask in the morning light for only a moment before I jump up at them, wildly waving my arms. "Shut up! I'm thinking! Get out of here! Bah!"

They love my tree too much for some reason and we are so used to each other's nuisances that they only scatter to higher branches rather than fleeing elsewhere. That seems to be our thing these days. They chirp too loudly, I shoo them, they stay, and I give up. But at least they've mostly quieted down.

"Alright, same time tomorrow?"

They chirp loudly in what I'd like to think is in response.

I turn around once again admitting defeat. "Cool. See you guys then."

A hot shower and four different shirts later I pour my coffee in a travel mug and head out. I take a sip of my delicious beverage as I start the car and begin to back out.

I take another sip when I slam on the brake. I scream out like a madman from the hot coffee taking a smooth spill on my chest.

I see my neighbor, Mr. Thompson, in the rearview mirror saying something with his fist in the air.

"Oh shit," I panic. I roll the window down. "What's that, Mr. Thompson?"

"I said you almost ran me over! Watch where you're going, son!" He walks on behind his walking group.

"S-Sorry, Mr. Thompson! I'll be careful next time!" He ignores me. That's okay. I didn't run him over and that's all that matters.

Before leaving for work I look down at the mess on my shirt, inspecting the level of damage. "Ehhh..." I shrug it off and decide that it probably isn't that bad.

I stop by the drive-thru of a local bakery and order something off of the spring menu, some sort of lavender-berry muffin. "Thank you," I say to the kind woman at the window.

"Enjoy your muffin," she says with sunshine in her tone.

"You as well," and I drive off. *You as well?* I breathe with exasperation, because what is this, my first time interacting with a customer service employee? Jeezus.

I make my way to the studio and the models we're photographing today are still getting their makeup done. Today, we are shooting for an influencer's merch. We love working with up-and-coming personalities because the energy is always so high and fun and never too serious, yet professional and usually know exactly what they want from us. It's always a good day when the client walks in with a vision.

Meanwhile, the part of me that used to be passionate about this work has burnt out. It's run its course. I don't get excited about it anymore. It's a good career path that I pursued since high school—photography club, shooting for the school paper, and apprenticing for a wedding photographer until the pressures of being a wedding photographer got the best of me and then finding Dean's studio and ultimately deciding to permanently join his team. Dean's studio is laid back compared to wedding season. The clients can certainly get interesting, and we have definitely gotten some interesting people, and we all get along—Dean, Karina, and me—even though I'm a decade younger than they are.

Despite the fun banter and playfulness going on, my mind is elsewhere. It wanders to what I might have for lunch and...

Do I have beer at home? I don't recall picking any up last week, so...I better pick some up just in case. I get to finally have my weekend beer and commence my weekend drinking. My weekend of lonely drinking. Unless Dean and Karina want to go to a karaoke bar like they mentioned wanting to do earlier this week. I don't know, Karina talked about doing ten different things this weekend.

I bring my train of thought to a screeching halt, realization hitting me. I'm with my coworkers too much. Maybe I need to re-download a dating app. Maybe I need to become passionate about someone, not something.

"Declan? Are you listening?"

My mind comes swiftly back to earth. "What? Sorry, I was..."

"Spaced out again?" Karina completes. She is our creative director. "Your angles are all wrong," she scolds. "Why don't you give me that camera and go take an early lunch, hm?"

I squint at her. "You're kicking me out?"

"Don't take it personally, friend. Go get your head cleared of whatever's going on in there and, uh, maybe buy a shirt from the gift shop or something. I wasn't going to say anything but..." She stares at the horror on my shirt. "Anyway, this will give me a little time with that camera of yours. Gimme gimme and get out of here."

"Okay then. I'm going to the cafe," I announce to everyone. "Does anybody want anything?"

Nobody does.

I leave for the cafe, as instructed, which is several floors down. I stare at the coffee stain in the reflection of the closed elevator doors. When the doors part, they reveal a woman. A gorgeous woman. Dark brunette hair, petite, and wearing dark red lipstick and is dressed in a stylish all black corporate outfit.

The doors start to close and my dumbass stays in place, letting it close on me. Thankfully, the gorgeous woman inside takes a quick step forward and sticks her hand through, keeping it open for me. "Are you coming in or...?" she asks considerately.

My soul returns to my body and I step inside. "Yeah,

sorry. I just...I was...I had something on my mind. I wasn't paying attention. My apologies." I wonder if she noticed that I was gawking and I cringe internally.

I don't have to press the button for the cafe floor. It's already pressed, making a mental note that we're going to get off on the same floor. I clasp my hands, waiting.

"Nice shirt," she says.

"Oh thanks," I reply. And in case she was sarcastically referring to the stain, I add, "Yeah, I had a little coffee spill this morning." Like an idiot, I turn around to give her a better look at it. Why? Because I'm a stupid dumb idiot.

Her eyes don't express any judgement. "I've had worse spills. I can be a clutz sometimes, too."

I want to explain to her why I spilled coffee on myself but then I would have to tell her that I almost ran my old neighbor over and I don't want to tell her that, and before I can come up with a pointless lie that she won't even care about, music plays. A familiar tune. I recognize it immediately to be H3H3's original intro from back when Ethan and Hila were making skits—way before their podcast.

Before I can wonder where the music is even coming from, the gorgeous woman pulls her phone out of her purse and greets the person on the other end. "Hey, I'm on my way there now. In the elevator."

And just like that, the music stopped. I turn back around, not minding her business, entertained that that's her ringtone.

From H3H3, the only OG Youtube creators that I still watch. My favorite Youtubers, cast included.

She drudged up that dusty old tune and made it her ringtone, never mind that nobody sets their ringtone anymore.

"Okay, see you in a bit. Bye." she ends her call.

Finally, after what feels like the longest elevator ride I've ever taken, the doors part at last. In slow motion, at least in my mind, I watch her, the most beautiful woman I've ever seen, walk out.

The doors close, taking me back up the building.

Shit. That was my floor.

CHAPTER 3

November

The only light now is from the TV until I flip the main light switch, blinding us. Our lazy day, other than having started a new commissioned cover art, has come to an end.

Liv gathers her things to leave. The rain has calmed but the wind tells me that there may be more to come and I'm not about to walk Liv out unprotected. Liv eyes me with a judgy brow as I put on a raincoat. "You're such a baby, you know that?"

"Girl, shut up. I'm going to take a post lazy day walk. I've got to walk off some of these snacks."

"In this drizzle?"

I nod with humorous pride. "Yeah well, I don't get this body by not pushing myself."

"Well shit, okay, Em."

"Right? You may apologize to me now."

She scoffs and walks out. “I need to move my body, too. We haven’t moved in hours.”

“I would have but you kept getting mad at me and ordering me to sit my ass down.”

She opens her car door. “Yeah, well, it was supposed to be a lazy day. I would have kept you from working if I was able to, making me feel behind on my work and all. Anyway, should we do something tomorrow?”

“Yeah, we should. How about our work?” I flash her a sarcastic smirk.

Liv rolls her eyes. “Oh, come on. Don’t you worry about me. You know I always get my shit done.”

That’s true, she just always loves to get it done at the very last minute and that makes me nervous. Doing it that way doesn’t leave us with a lot of extra time to look things over twenty times. “Right. We’ll see how we feel tomorrow.”

“That’s November code for I don’t want to do anything but work.”

I close the car door on her and wave, ready for her to leave. “Bye. Drive safe.”

“Talk to you later, doll.” She drives off.

I put in my earbuds and browse through YouTube as I start my walk. The wind blows flurries of rain on my face, my hood useless against the sideways flurries.

I put on a new H3 Podcast episode about Hila getting sued, desperately trying to ignore the cold splatters on my face.

I walk for fifteen minutes through my sleepy neighborhood spotlit by streetlights, walking the glittering blacktop with the familiar breeze that alerts me that more rain is about to hit as gusts of wind blow through the inside of my coat, giving me goosebumps. A chill runs up my spine and I pick up my pace.

Another gust of wind hit a tree at the perfect time I'm walking underneath it and water droplets hit me everywhere. Not long after that, the sky skips the part where it slowly progresses and goes straight to downpouring. I run but am instantly drenched. I run faster, wanting out of this freezing hell.

Minutes later, I see the blinking streetlight right outside my house—I've never been so happy to see my broken, flickering light—which signals to me that I'm close. Closer to getting out of these sopping wet clothes and shoes and into a nice warm fluffy robe. Closer to drinking hot chocolate under a warm blanket. Closer to falling asleep as a cozy horror show plays in the background. Ah, yes. I'm almost there.

I'm nearing my neighbor's house, not Helena's, when I take out my earbuds and put them in the case, still running. When I make it inside I grab a kitchen towel to dry them off. I open the case to take them out but one is missing.

Confusion hits, as I could swear that I put them both in the case, then search the floor at the entryway. I feel inside my pockets. And then I search my pockets and the floor five more times.

"Fuuuck," I groan. I probably dropped it trying to put

them in the case, and now it's somewhere out there getting rained on. I need to find it. I really don't want to buy another set. This is my second pair this year. I lost my first pair in a city two hours away when Liv and I went to one of our author's events to show our support, and I didn't realize they were missing until I was home unpacking.

I run back outside in the dreadful rain and look all around the pavement. I stomp my feet in the puddles hoping to feel it, and the moment I touch it...

Boom! Thunder and lightning strike right over me, too loud and too bright at the same time. My vision goes white. I lose all sound completely, except for a faint ringing in my ears.

When the ringing fades, silence.

My fingers close around the earbud and I slowly straighten myself upright. Only, now there's no rain at all. No puddles. Nothing is wet.

I look down at myself.

Except me. I'm soaked while everything around me looks like it hasn't been touched by rain at all.

I look up at the sky. It's a clear night, save for the small wispy clouds.

Slowly, I turn around, inspecting my surroundings. Inspecting my...neighborhood? This *is* still my neighborhood, isn't it?

It still looks like Everglow but...different? I do a full 360, taking in the details of this place, questioning some unfamiliar differences when my eyes unexpectedly meet with a man's, who is staring back at me. He is frozen in place from pulling out some grocery bags from the back seat of his car. Beer, to be exact. Two six-packs to be *exact* exact.

We both stand stiffly. Unmoving. While I can probably guess that my eyes show absolute confusion, his eyes show what looks like...shock? Fear? Like he's looking at a ghost. A monster. I look around me once more. No ghost. No monster. Just us.

We gawk at each other for what feels like a long time before realizing that this man doesn't live at this house. Maybe he's a guest of the house? Because that's not the homeowner's vehicle either.

I look over at my own house. It looks like my house, only...the streetlight is no longer flickering, perfectly lit with a white light, not yellow.

I can't stand the silence anymore, nor the hundreds of questions swirling at the tip of my tongue all at once.

Finally, I suck in a breath and dare to be the one to say something. "What is—"

" —THIS?"

In an instant I'm back in the rain in the Everglow that I know. As rain continues to heavily pour, my breathing quickens with panic. My chest rises and falls fast by the second.

The clear sky is gone. The man with the two six-packs of beer is gone. Everything is wet again.

I run back to my house and I don't strip off my clinging clothes like I planned. I don't get into my fuzzy robe like I planned. Hot cocoa doesn't even exist in my mind by this point.

I pull out my phone and frantically try to navigate to Liv's contact. The phone screen is wet, my fingers are wet, and my phone is having a hard time understanding what I'm trying to do.

Thankfully, at least Liv doesn't take forever to answer. "Yo."

"Liv!" I shriek. "Liv, I-I—" My entire body shakes so hard that I trip over my own foot and drop the phone, though I continue to yell at it as I try to keep my grip on it. "I think I just had a fucking stroke! What the fuck. What the fuck! I don't know what just fucking happened but something happened!"

"What? A stroke? Girl, stop playing and just say what you're trying to say. I'm still on the road and you're going to get me into an accident."

"A stroke! Or...some sort of psychosis or...some sort of delirium...from a bad fever, maybe. I don't know but I swear! I fucking swear. I-I was walking. Remember? I told you I was going for a walk. Remember? So, I was walking," I repeat. My words aren't coming out the way I mean for them to.

"And then...it rained. And then the lightning was so fucking bright. Did you see that bright ass lightning? It was so bright I couldn't see anything, and then when I could see again, I wasn't here! Or like, I was still here but I wasn't *here* here."

I know what this sounds like but I keep going anyway while everything is still fresh and vivid. "And it was raining but everything was dry and..." Oh my god, I sound crazy. "There was a man! Next door! But I've never seen him before. And my streetlight..."

Give up, November. Just give up already. "Ugh," I groan in defeat.

Liv doesn't say anything but I can feel her eyes squinting, trying to put the pieces together to form a full coherent picture of what I'm failing so badly to provide. "Okay, wait... so...it was...wet? And then...it was dry? Or..." I know she has to be cringing at the way she attempts to repeat what I had just word vomited.

I moan in horrific embarrassment and cover my face with my hands. "Ugh, yes but..."

She certainly picks up on my wanting to give up on this conversation. "No! I'm sorry, tell me again. I'm not sure I heard you very well. I'm on the road and I wasn't really... focusing on what you were saying. Sorry. Go ahead."

I plop on the sofa, facedown. "Uggghhh, never mind. I sound crazy."

"November, you need to tell me, did you have a stroke or something? Did something happen? Do I need to call an ambulance? Do you need me to turn around? I"ll turn around if you need me."

My shoulders slump, my energy suddenly depleted. "No. No ambulance, no turning around." I breathe in deeply and start over. "So...after you drove off..." I walk Liv through this unbelievable story, detail by detail, and she listens without judgement, at least not out loud. Surely she has to be making silent judgements. By the end, she doesn't know how to appropriately respond. I know she wants to make jokes but I know she's keeping herself from doing so as I am in a state of distress and it in fact is not as serious as needing an ambulance.

I hear that she finally makes it home. I can hear her keys jingling and unlocking the door. I can hear her putting her things down and rummaging in the kitchen. I hear anything else but what she makes of my little tale. "Are you going to say something? I mean, I don't know what to make of it either."

"I think...that your hatred for rain probably triggered something different in you tonight. At least that's what it sounds like to me, anyway." I agree with her to get this conversation over with. "Because what else could it have been? Obviously you didn't enter into another universe or anything like that, so..." she trails off.

"Yeah, of course. You're right." She can't be right, though. I'm not crazy about my disdain for this weather but I know what I saw and I know what I felt.

I strip my clothes off and towel myself dry and fish out

my fluffy robe from the closet. I wrap my hair in a towel and make some cocoa. Even though Liv is wrong, I have to convince myself that she is right. I need to believe her, because what would be the alternative? Mull over it for the rest of my life?

CHAPTER 4

Declan

First, I lost my breath in the face of her striking beauty. Then she spoke, her voice silky and mellifluous, and stole my entire consciousness like a thief in the night. Third, her gentle kindness for the sole reason that she couldn't help herself. Finally, her ringtone was the final blow. The ringtone that told me that she's someone with humor and easy vibes.

And just like that, I was hers.

Of course I didn't interpret it that way when I got back to the office.

"So, an attractive woman compliments you, stain and all, and you couldn't find the nerve to ask for her name?" Karina asks, appalled and shaking her head in disappointment. "That's rough. Who knows if that'll ever happen to you again. Sorry, friend."

I busy my hands wiping down all the camera gear,

regretting my little story time. "Wow, thanks. I appreciate your support and confidence. Truly."

"I mean that with love. You know I love you but you don't go anywhere, you don't do anything unless it's with us. You don't even have your dating app anymore."

My face scrunches. "How do you know that?"

"Don't worry about that. All I'm saying is if you're not looking, fine, but it sounds like there could have been a connection there and you let that opportunity slip out of your hands like a slimy fish flopping its way back to water."

"You let the fish get away," Dean says. He is the only married one here. "You know how they say there's plenty of fish in the sea? Well, there's only one soulmate and you can't afford to let chances slip away. Don't let that fish swim too far away, Declan."

Karina sneers at his sarcasm. "I know he's being silly about it but he's right. She could have been the one and you let her off the hook so carelessly."

"Okay, can we stop talking about her like she's a fish? I keep picturing her as a fish now."

"Right. Well, good work today. Everything turned out great, looked good, and went smoothly. They were very happy with everything. Let's get dinner and celebrate. I'm starving." Dean rubs his gut.

I pack away my gear and set them in the closet and lock it up. "Nah, I think I'll pass this time. Sorry, guys."

"My wife will be disappointed if you're not there. You know how much she loves seeing the two of you. She's been building up stories to tell you for next time." He turns to Karina. "Don't tell her I've already told you if things start to sound familiar."

"Dean, you know it's always a pleasure seeing Olivia but I don't know, I feel like I've been in a funk all day."

"Try these last couple of weeks," Karina chimes under her breath.

"I don't know what it is and I can't shake it off. Can I make it up to you tomorrow? Yeah, let's do something tomorrow. How's that sound?"

"You kids and your social batteries," Dean shames, shaking his head.

But Karina's eyes light up. "Let's go book shopping! Please!"

"Yes yes, we can do that tomorrow. Right, Dean?"

Dean nods. "Yes, of course. It'll beat going to karaoke. I seriously can't hang like that anymore."

"Cool. I'll text you later, Karina. Or you can text me. Doesn't matter. You guys have fun at dinner and I'll see you tomorrow."

"Okay, feel better, Declan," Karina says.

I'm still not sure if I have beer at the house. If I do, there probably won't be more than a couple, so I better stop by somewhere and get more.

I stop at a gas station, fill up on gas, and grab a couple of six-packs.

Before pulling into my driveway I make sure to take extra care to look around for pedestrians, specifically Mr.

Thompson, and especially now that the sun is gone. I also want to avoid exchanging words with the old man.

The coast is clear and I get out of the car, whistling a random tune, excited to start my weekend doing nothing but making myself a juicy steak and potatoes and drinking a few beers and watching a horror movie. As I pull out the cases of beer I jump at the sound of a loud crack, and out of nowhere...

A woman. Where the hell did she come from?

She was not here, or anywhere, literally a second ago. Water drips heavily from her head all the way down to her shoes. And what the hell did that god awful sound come from?

She faces me now and I can't get myself to blink. I don't know what to do. My eyes burn from keeping my eyes open, drying up. I consciously remind myself to close my eyelids.

It's her—the woman from the elevator. Or at least it looks like her. I'm not certain, because this is impossible. This person materializing out of nowhere is impossible. So what the hell am I seeing?

"What is—"

And just like that, she is gone.

My heart does a somersault at the sight of her vanishing right before my eyes. *What is.* That's what she said. What is that supposed to mean? Where did she go? Where did she come from? How did she get here? Why was she here? Why was she soaked? What just happened?!

I calmly enter my house and place the beers in the refrigerator but take one. I peek out of the window. There is clear evidence that my eyes have not deceived me. My brain was not malfunctioning. The puddle she left behind is still there. I sit on the porch, then immediately get back up and pace around the water spot. I take a photo of it with my phone, not like it proves or explains anything to anyone, but I guess just to keep the proof for myself because right now I am questioning my cognitive state.

I go back inside and start on my dinner, but every few minutes I look out of the kitchen window in case she comes back—the woman who looks like the one from the elevator.

This has to be a glitch in the matrix. A mistake from the universe. A misconception and correction by destiny.

Waiting for the potatoes to boil, I pull up the photo and there it still is.

Why her, though? Why does she look like a woman I just met today? She didn't recognize me. Then again, why would she recognize a man who she had a brief exchange of words with for less than a couple of minutes?

I, however, recognized her pretty much immediately, because she is undoubtedly recognizable, what with her beauty. Her stunning allure.

I quietly thank the universe for a glimpse of the most beautiful woman ever. I don't understand it but I think I found my new passion. Many thoughts swirl around my mind. Pictures are forming, too quickly to process. A glimpse of her...with me. Of a future together.

A glimpse of us.

CHAPTER 5

November

My eyes stir when I hear something, and then I hear it again. Knocks on my door. It takes effort to open my heavy eyes. My fingers rub them awake and I wait for my vision to focus. More knocks. I check my phone for the time and I'm right, it's definitely too early. Eight-forty-five on a Saturday. Someone must hate me. I wonder if it's Helena.

I see some texts from Liv. One says good morning and that she is going to pick up breakfast and asks if I have juice for mimosas. The second text says to forget her previous text and she will just pick some up and Eren wants to tag along so he'll be coming over as well. And of course she adds that she thinks that's a wonderful idea.

My phone vibrates. Liv is calling. "Hey, Liv," I answer without clearing the frog in my throat.

"Hey, sleepyhead. We're here. I'm guessing you were still asleep since you never responded to my texts. How are you doing this morning? Are you feeling okay? Feeling any better?"

"Yeah," I croak, rolling out of bed to open the door for them. "I slept hard but I think I had some weird dreams or something. I don't know. I have a slight headache."

"Awe, I'm sorry, love. But since we're here, we'll take care of you."

I open the door but still speak into the phone. "Are you guys sure you want to be here? I'm very low energy right now."

Though Liv is staring back at me, she also continues to speak into the phone. "We're not going anywhere. Isn't that right, Eren?" she shouts behind her.

Eren is collecting the grocery bags and restaurant bags and walks up the porch. "Thanks for your help, Liv."

"Hi, Eren" I say into the phone.

"Oh, hold on real quick." Liv turns to Eren and holds the phone out to him. "November wants to say hi to you."

We watch Eren very seriously until he puts his mouth to the speaker of the phone. "Hi, Em. May we please come in? There's food in these bags and I'm starving."

Liv and I burst into laughter. "Yes, come in. Welcome to my house and make yourself at home, Eren."

"Why don't you freshen up and we'll set up breakfast," Liv suggests.

"Sure, thanks." I close myself in the bathroom and wait for the water to warm up. I look at the wet clothes in my basket and a memory from last night flashes in my mind.

The flash of white, the loud boom of thunder, the man next door. When I cup water to my face an image of myself flashes next, like I'm seeing myself through an out of body experience. I convince myself that whatever that was, there was no doubting the impossibility.

It wasn't real.

It wasn't real.

It wasn't real.

When I make my way to the dining table, Liv and Eren are already digging into the bacon, eggs, and french toast. My plate is made and a fresh hot coffee awaits me beside it. I take a seat beside Eren. "You guys are so good to me. What on earth did I do to deserve this?" I take a bite of french toast first.

Eren wipes his mouth with a napkin and swallows his food before answering. "Liv said you were feeling under the weather. She wanted to cheer you up and asked if I wanted to tag along."

I look at my best friend, sitting across from me, when he says *under the weather*, my eyes silently asking if she told him about my...hallucination. She shakes her head subtly and I believe her, I guess. How can one not gossip about such a tale? I don't know, but I'm glad for it.

"So what's wrong? Are you sick?"

"Or have a stroke?" Liv teases, sipping her coffee. The joke goes over Eren's head, of course. He doesn't look up from his food or question it at all.

I raise a brow slightly in Liv's direction. "No, Liv, I did

not have a stroke. And I'm not too sick or anything. I simply went for a nighttime walk thinking that I could get back before the rain hit again, but I got caught in a nasty downpour and caught a little cold last night. Hence why I hate it when it rains. It tries to kill me every time."

"Awe, you're a delicate little flower, aren't you?" Eren teases as he boops my nose, thinking nothing of it, continuing to chow down.

I glower at him, ignoring his playful smile and Liv's raised brows, not bothering to hide her astonishment. She has been advocating for this since she first introduced us a year ago and she's finally seeing something of a baby step.

"I'm feeling much better, especially with my own personal DoorDash."

"Anytime," he says."

"I meant Liv, actually."

"Of course. Well, you can call me from now on. I promise I'll give better service," he says with a wink that catches me off guard.

My face grows hot and Liv still hasn't relaxed the muscles in her face.

He gets up and clears Liv's and his plates and clangs around the kitchen to start making mimosas.

Liv and I share different silent reactions. I am utterly flustered and she has a hand cupped to her mouth, the two of us sitting in our frozen expressions.

I pretend to pick at my food but the butterflies in my stomach are too excited and lively to keep an appetite. Eren has been doing that a lot lately, making obvious comments like that towards me, and if it's to make his intentions clear, well, they're crystal. I just don't know that I have the mind to date at the moment.

Liv gets up and leaves the table. "Where are you going?" I panic.

She looks at me with an aversion to my desperate question. "To the bathroom, you freak."

After she walks out of ear shot he brings over the mimosas and takes his seat. "I don't know how you deal with her. She's such a bully."

"I shrug. "Eh, but a sweet bully."

"Sweet? She bullied me into driving her around even though she's the one that invited me to tag along."

"That's our Liv," I say with another shrug.

Neither of us said anything for a while. I kept hoping Liv would appear second after second and when she never did I could feel the awkward tension grow. "So how's the new job been treating you?"

He takes a sip of his mimosa. "It's been good. Better. Bartending at a classy restaurant beats bartending at a shitty one. The tips are better. I don't get yelled at by drunk assholes. Less throw up throughout the week. The bathrooms stay cleaner all week long. Yeah, it's been so much better. How about you? What's it been like living the dream working your dream job with your dream partner?"

"It's a dream," I laugh. "Truly. I can work in nothing but my underwear if I want, and I have." I regret that enthusiastic comment straight away. This is a typical thing that I say to Liv. It doesn't exactly hit the same way saying it to a man.

Eren doesn't avert his gaze, which makes me blush. I wonder if he is really imagining me working in nothing but my underwear or if he is merely waiting for me to continue.

I laugh it off and take a long gulp of my mimosa.

Liv finally returns. "Em, I took the liberty of putting your drenched clothes from last night in the wash. Man, you must have—Oh damn, are you alright? You look flushed."

Oh, good grief. Shut up, Liv. "It's the mimosa. I must be drinking too quickly. I'm good, though."

"Seriously, though, if you really feel, uh, unwell, just say the word and we can get out of your hair."

"I'm okay. Really." Changing the subject, I ask, "Do you guys want to start Poldark with me?"

Liv scrunches her face. "What the fuck is a Poldark?"

"It's a historical fiction on Netflix. I saw the preview and, I don't know, it looks awfully romantic. It looks like it's riddled with drama."

"No, thank you. Let's binge something else."

Eren is already cozy on the living room chair. "Uh, excuse you, Liv, but Em is the sick one, remember? We're here to cater to her."

"Uggghhh fine. Put it on."

"Oh don't be such a baby, Liv," I shove her shoulder. "We'll watch a couple episodes and if we're not feeling it after that, we'll watch something else. Deal?"

"Yeah, yeah," she grumbles.

In the first episode, Poldark comes back from war after three years to find that his love, who he left behind, has thought him dead and moves on to none other than a close cousin of his. The longing in their eyes, the regret, the yearning knowing that they can no longer have each other, the ache of seeing each other and not being able to hold each other...what must that feel like, I wonder.

Watching Ross Poldark and Elizabeth try to move on with their lives over the next few episodes—they were absolutely tortured. Tormented. Distraught.

It is heartbreakingly beautiful.

CHAPTER 6

Declan

A TEXT FROM KARINA AWAKENS ME. SHE LECTURES ME ABOUT NOT texting her about any solid plans for today and I better not back out. I'm about to respond to lecture *her* for texting *me* so damn early but it's already nine-thirty.

Typically, I'm an early bird on the weekends. Early morning coffees are mandatory, water before a run, and then spend some time in my office before a shower. I haven't slept like this in a very long time. I don't think I stayed up that late, keeping a lookout for another weird incident, but I guess I must have. I don't even recall dozing off.

I tell Karina and Dean our plans for later. I'll pick her up before dinnertime and we'll hit up a Barnes and Noble. Dean and Olivia can meet us there and after shopping I'll take her to get some Chinese takeout and then take her home.

Dean responds first, that he will meet us there but Olivia is going to be at her parents' house tonight, though she gave him a list of books that she wants him to get for her. Karina isn't too pleased that I didn't plan anything more. She is disappointed that I don't plan on having dinner or drinks with her. I explain to her that I want to be back in time for the golden hour. I want to take some photos to update my personal photo accounts on social media.

There's a pretty little spot near my house where when the sunlight hits just right, it lights up the lonely tree and turns into art. If you have the magic eye, that is. To a person who doesn't have a creative bone in their body, it could appear to them as an ordinary tree, one stunted in its growth and spruce in blossoms. I call it the Kingdom of Flowers. It's a bit of an oxymoron. It's really not the most gorgeous place, but I am one to appreciate beauty in the odd, the awkward, and dare I say the unsightly.

I have a late coffee on the porch and replay that odd occurrence from last night. I thought about it all night and now I'm realizing that all sound vanished. The noise from my neighbor's backyard barbeque completely ceased. The crickets were completely muted. The whoosh of wind through the trees or any white noise, removed.

Mr. Thompson walks by with his walking group and their chatter cuts through my thoughts. I wave at him and, to my surprise, when he glances over he waves back. I am relieved to know that he doesn't hate me for nearly killing him, a man in his sixties.

The relief is nice and gives me the burst of energy I need. I begin to clean my house. I start by doing a load of laundry while I finish listening to H3's podcast episode from yesterday. It makes me think of the woman from the elevator. I think of the way her dark hair was clipped back as strands fell loose on her forehead. Her stylish black blazer. The golden pendant of her necklace that rested on her black blouse. Her big doll eyes that more than likely did notice my gawking.

She fills my mind until Karina and I make it to the bookstore and I realize that I wasn't present for our conversations. I would feel bad if she wasn't carrying the conversation all on her own for the whole trip here.

Once inside, we gravitate to our separate genres. I find myself thinking of her again. I end up in the romance section and behold a book cover where two characters embrace each other in their arms. I imagine the beautiful stranger and I holding each other and idly creating a love story of us. Something sweet that we can someday tell to our children and grandchildren.

I absentmindedly continue to slowly trail down aisle after aisle, faking interest in a book every now and then, picking it up, not reading the synopsis, and staring blankly at it, and then putting it back on the shelf.

I'm at the end of another aisle and about to enter a new one, when suddenly...

I see her.

Our eyes meet at the same time, they grow wide with astonishment in the same way. We both smile, yet neither of us want to smile too eagerly. Eventually, we both catch on to that and smile brightly and shyly through the awkwardness.

"Hey," I hope I say coolly. "It's you."

"And you. Hi. Uh, fancy meeting you here." The gorgeous elevator stranger takes in my attire. "You clean up nicely."

I stifle a laugh. "Thanks. You too."

Her brows furrow, surely remembering that she looked immaculate yesterday.

"I mean, you looked beautiful before. And now, too, you're beautiful. You still are beautiful. I mean, I'm sure you always look beautiful." I desperately wish I could stop saying she's beautiful.

"You think I'm beautiful?" she blushes. She asks it as if she doesn't already know it herself, but there's no way she doesn't.

It's nice to see her smile at the embarrassing amount of times I said the word beautiful in a span of like five seconds.

"I'm sorry—are you joking?"

Again, her brows furrow.

I gesture at her whole self. "Look at you." I can't find any more words than that at this instant.

"And look at you. No coffee stain."

"Oh, thanks. That's very gracious of you to notice. Yeah, sometimes I can look like a functioning adult."

"Just sometimes, right?"

"Just sometimes, yeah," I agree.

When we're done laughing, neither of us want to be the one to speak next. In my case, I don't want to seem like I want to keep her, even though I want all of her time, but if she has things to do I don't want her to feel like she has to entertain a conversation with me. Though, even in this moment of not speaking, I am enjoying how our eyes lock into each other's, comfortable in each other's gazes.

"I'm Declan," I finally say. I hold out my hand.

"I'm November." She takes my hand gently. My thumb brushes her skin, hopefully not noticeably. I can't help myself. But if she does notice, she doesn't let on.

"November." I savor her name on my lips for the first time. "That's a beautiful name."

"You really need to choose a different word to use or it'll start to go to my head."

I notice that she looks at our hands, still holding onto the handshake. I let her go. "I'm a big fan of your season."

"Aaand there it is."

"There what is?"

"I definitely don't get that a lot, and especially not all my life." She smiles teasingly.

"Damn. And here I thought I was being clever. So, why November? Where does that come from?"

"Well, the short story is that November is my mother's favorite month."

"And the long story?"

She hesitates. I watch her smile fade, and then come back. "My father passed away some time during my mother's pregnancy. She grieved for...forever. Still is, to be honest, even though she won't admit that to me or my stepfather.

People usually guess that I was born in November and that's why my name is November. I wasn't. It's the month my parents got married."

I can tell that, in a way, she loves telling the story of her name. There's a glee in her smile as she tells it and it fills me with giddiness. "Wow. While I am sorry for your loss, that is such a...heartbreakingly beautiful story."

"Okay, now you're messing with me."

I tilt my head in question.

"You're about to be cut off from that word." She crosses her arms.

I'm still so enamored by the origin of her name before realizing what she means. I shrug. I can't tell her that that word has hardly been in my regular vocabulary even with my line of work. I don't typically say a model is beautiful or is doing beautifully. I'd instead say that the shot looks awesome or call a model pose perfect. Or even with my landscape photographs where I'd typically describe a scenery as amazing, awesome, or wonderful. Not beautiful.

Until you. I wipe my face with a hand in embarrassment. "Yeah...I'll stop," I laugh. I won't say it anymore. I won't say it out loud how beautiful she is. How beautiful her voice sounds. How beautiful her soul feels. How beautifully she tells the story of her name.

She smirks. "I mean, you can say it, just...now, I'll make fun of you for it. I'll keep a mental counter."

"Oh gosh, no. Don't do that," I chuckle. "But seriously,

it's touching how your mother commemorated your father in that way. Thank you for sharing the long version."

"From the way my mother still talks about him, even to this day, I hope to someday meet someone that has the same effect on me." Her words hang awkwardly over our heads. "Oh damn. I probably shouldn't have said that, huh?" Her cute little button nose scrunches, holding back a smile. "Oh god, that was awkward of me to say."

While she laughs about it I simply shake my head in disagreement, still smiling and wanting her to continue to talk that way. I could listen to it all day. I *want* to listen to it all day. I want to know more of what she wants. I want to be the one to give it to her.

In my peripheral view I see a Dean-shaped figure and turn my head. It is Dean. He finally made it. He points at me and I hear him say, "Ah, there he is."

A single moment later Karina stands beside him and sees me. Her eyes dart back and forth from myself and the woman she seems to be surprised to see me talking to. "Nope. That ain't him, stupid," shoving Dean out of my sight.

Children, they are! I don't realize that my eyes are shut in embarrassment from having been caught talking to a woman and being pointed at by my friends. I try not to react in front of November to them pretending like they don't know me. I don't know what to do with that.

I definitely don't want to part ways with her for them, but I did plan this day with them, for them. Well, for Karina.

She looks at me with curiosity. "Uh, friends of yours?"

Karina and Dean are now behind November. Karina is mouthing to me to stay with her and she will go off with Dean.

I try not to look too distracted but November turns around. When she turns, Karina and Dean look anywhere else but at her and eventually just leave the store.

I don't know what to do. I try to look as confused as she does. "Uh, no. I don't know those weirdos."

Her smirk tells me that she doesn't believe me but goes along with it anyway. She knows something is up. She probably knows those not-my-friends weirdos know that she is filling my stomach with butterflies. What, does she want me to say it? I'm not about to tell her that I feel like I'm in a movie. Boy meets girl. Boy wants to cup girl's face in his hands. Girl tells him to kiss her already.

I want to tell her that I don't need to get to know her—that I feel like I already do. Her eyes tell me every single time I get lost in them. They tell me that she's my wife. Just not yet.

CHAPTER 7

November

OVER THE NEXT MONTH, WHENEVER I WOULD RUN BY MY neighbor's house, I would always relive that odd night. The man I saw during that supposed delirious fever dream, I have yet to see him or his little red Subaru at this house.

A small family lives here—a couple in their thirties or forties and a middle school kid and a small little white curly-haired fur baby with buttons for eyes—they own a dark grey van of some sort, not a red Subaru. They moved here not that much longer after me and we have never really exchanged words, just the occasional wave and I passed candy out to them last year on Halloween. They seem like nice people but I'm a single woman and something of a recluse whose other neighbor likes to lecture her for exercising in her sports bra or comment on watering her flower bushes or remind her to not let the grass get too long during the summer.

Anyway, no sign of the man from my delirium.

However, my alarm bells ring when I see Helena come out of her house. It's like she stands at her window waiting for me to come home. Gee, I wonder if it's because I'm in my sports bra again. I sprint to my door but she also sprints to catch me. I groan. "Helena, I'm sorry for my sports bra again but it feels better when—"

She waves my words away, though she's cringing at my exposed chest and midsection. "No, sweetie, no. I'm not here for that. I understood you plainly last time." A hint of shame or embarrassment surfaces on Helena's face. Guilt bubbles in my stomach. "You need to water your yard, dear. Your plants." She gestures to the surrounding houses. "Look, everyone else is taking care of their lawn and unfortunately yours is beginning to stick out like a sore thumb, my dear," she tittered.

I don't stop walking when she meets me at the front of my house. "Oh okay, you're right. I'll be sure to do that. I appreciate you for reminding me."

"W-Would you like to join me and the ladies for some tea? Coffee? Oh! I made some cookies! They're perfect, I swear!"

"No, it's okay. I have plans. Thank you, though." I close the door on her and hurry into the shower. I don't have a *date* date with Eren, but it's lunch. He invited me to hang out with him during his lunch break and I figured why not. I don't mind getting out of the house once in a while and pretend like I have a life. Rotting away in my cave staring at a screen for hours a day can't be the healthiest thing for anyone to do.

I put on a new episode of H3 Podcast that I missed on Friday as background noise as I get ready. I text Liv to triple check that she can't join us for lunch. She claims that she still can't. She is swamped with client work. I text back lecturing her about not having done it sooner. She retorts with heart emojis and encourages me to have fun.

She's been laying her romantic hints between Eren and me real thick lately. His crush on me has lasted long and with no end in sight. I would be lying if I said that I haven't imagined what dating Eren would be like, especially when comparing it to my last dumpster fire of a relationship with Miles. The snake had been extra loving toward me a week after I moved out of Liv's place and into my own little oasis, my current house, and asked if he could move in with me and out of his own friend's place. Naturally, I thought it would be a good idea to take us and our relationship to the next stage, and I should have known better. By that point, we had known each other for almost a year from working together at a grocery store. I should have known better when during the whole first week of living together he had quit the store job for something more fulfilling. The issue was that nothing fulfilled him. He wasn't motivated to do a goddamn thing. He was a mooch and one day I decided that I couldn't take it anymore and called up his friend to help him pack and take him back.

Needless to say it was not a clean breakup and it left me

scarred. I've been afraid of commitment ever since. Eren may look put together and seem sweet and nice and all the good things now, but as I've learned, that can all change the moment he starts to get what he wants from me, whatever that may be. From my ugly ex, it was anything he could get. Anything I was willing to give from my heart while he gave me nothing but empty promises of doing the bare minimum, like getting a job or cleaning after himself or going to bed with me during the week.

Before I know it, I'm stepping out of the elevator to the floor of his restaurant to let Eren know I'm here. He's talking with a couple of waiters when he spots me walking in. "Hey, you," he says as he comes closer and closer to me until I'm enveloped in his arms. The younger waiters share a smile that silently says something to one another and walk away as they speak in hushed tones. He points behind me and says, "I'll meet you over there at the snack shop. I need to do one thing and then we'll have like twenty minutes."

I look behind me, confused. "Wait, so we're not having lunch here?"

"Nah, there's no break room and I don't want to risk getting caught sitting around."

"But you'd be on break."

"Yeah, tell me about it." He turns me around and lightly shoves me forward. "I can't be caught fraternizing. I'll be there soon."

"Okay, okay. I'll order something for us. Don't be long," I

demand, since he sends me away like I'm a child badgering him at work.

I make a mental note to tell Eren and Liv that I want to eat in that restaurant sometime. The dim lighting in the daylight screams fancy. The black tie staff attire screams class and it's been a while since I have gone someplace where there wasn't a drive-thru. And when I'm not at a drive-thru, Liv brings me food.

While I wait to order I think about the way he took me in his arms. I can swear he was aware of the perfume on my neck or inhaled the scent of my shampoo. And the light way his nose brushed my cheek as we pulled apart.

I think about the way his eyes lit up when he saw me, just like Liv told me before, and how one side of his mouth curled up. Maybe it's time for me to explore a new relationship. I mean, what am I going to do? Be single forever? That sounds miserable.

I order us both the same thing—a deviled egg sandwich, a bag of chips, and a bottle of water. I step aside to wait for my order. I mindlessly scroll through Instagram when suddenly I feel an odd sensation in my head and behind my eyes, a sort of pulsing and burning. I close my eyes, try to focus on my breathing and try not to panic. The pressure reminds me of a migraine but without the pain. I wonder if I can ignore it or if I need to lie down or run to the bathroom to throw up. I don't know what effect it's giving me exactly. I continue to inhale air slowly through my nose and push it out of my lungs, desperately trying to gain control.

I rub my fingers at my temples, swirling over and over.

I swirl...until I notice that all sound has gone. All but my own breathing.

I open my eyes. I'm standing in an empty cafe. The lights flicker. I look all around me. This is familiar. My heart races, realizing that the same thing happened a month ago and it's happening again. Happening now. Happening with my eyes wide open, happening with a clear head. This is really happening. It was real then and it's real now.

I close my eyes once more with the intention of going back to where I just was. Where I really am, not this...this alternate place.

Bring me back. Bring me back. I don't want to be here. Bring me back.

I don't know how long I repeat this in my head but I think it again and again, until I hear another voice.

"Ma'am? Ma'am, your order," says a bodiless voice.

I keep blinking until I see a woman handing me my food.

I'm back. I look around and the cafe isn't empty anymore. "Sorry, thank you." I take the tray and turn around to look for an open table. Though when I turn, my eyes connect with a man that looks like the one from my fever dream. It's been some time since the incident but his face was pretty memorable. I walk by as slowly and discreetly as I can.

But not as discreetly as I think I am. "Uh, can I help you?"

I don't realize my gawking at him. Yet, upon further

gawking, his features morph into someone else entirely and no longer looks familiar at all.

I play back my fever dream—the man taking his beer out of his car, the shock on his face—I try hard to match this face to that and I don't know how I was grossly mistaken. They don't look alike at all. "Sorry, I...I thought you were someone else."

I must be seeing things. There's no way I should be able to remember a stranger from one fever dream. He can't be real.

When I take a seat, someone takes a seat with me, and it's not Eren. It's... "Miles," I blurt with a crack in my voice.

"Hey, babe. Wow, I–" he combs his hair back out of his face, " –what are you doing here?" He seems genuinely happy to have run into me. I must say, it feels nice. This is the sort of giddiness I wanted when we were together.

"I'm here to have lunch with a friend." Right as I said that my heart begins to pound, nervous for some reason I can't explain that he's going to catch me with another man.

"Oh shit, is Liv with you? I miss that girl. Just a little though."

I let out an exasperated breath. "I can't say that the feeling would be mutual. But no, I'm not here to meet with Liv."

His head tilts out of confusion and I know exactly what that's about. He probably can't process the notion of me having another friend, one who is not Liv.

Suddenly, Eren is here. He leans on the table, his attention on me. "Hey, hope you didn't have to wait too long." His head turns to Miles. "Sup, buddy."

"Eren, this is Miles."

Eren turns to me again, a smirk forming. Then he faces Miles again and lets out a snarky chortle. "Ah. Heard a lot about you, man. Good to meet you." He sticks out his hand. When Miles takes it, Eren grips him and pulls him up and out of the booth. "Sorry, man. My breaks aren't very long and, uh, we've got plans."

Miles smirks sarcastically and re-centers the neckline of his shirt. "Yeah, sure. Call me sometime, babe. I miss you."

I grunt, embarrassed. "Don't call me babe, Miles. And you know I'm not going to call you."

I hear a woman's voice call out for Miles at the entrance. When he reaches her I hear him tell her that he doesn't want to eat here anymore.

Once he's gone, Eren and I share entertained looks. His unserious smile spreads warmth through my chest, and I know that I have to try to put my fever dream to rest. Maybe all it is is my mind trying to tell me that I'm ready to open my heart and let someone in. The least I can do is try and give Eren a chance, whatever that may look like.

CHAPTER 8

Declan

THE GREATEST THING I EVER DID WAS SPILL COFFEE ON MYSELF that day. Because of that, a beautiful woman noticed me. Because of her, I have floated into the clouds. Floated far away, from an emptiness I was beginning to feel. Instead of wondering if I have beers in the fridge, I wonder if she'll join me for one. Instead of wondering if I should update my dating profile, I wonder when I should ask her out. Instead of being dragged to doing what Karina wants, I want to be dragged to doing everything November wants.

I have had the best weeks of my life bumping into her around the building. Her compliments of my clothes, my hair, give me confidence I didn't know I have. I hunger for her voice every single day. I fucking need it. I pine for her searching eyes until they find mine. I find it hard to focus on work. On chores. On keeping in touch with my mother and friends. All I do is hold the image of us at the bookstore, where it was your typical running-into-each-other romance movie scene. And all these weeks, I've been sitting in the front row of my own movie watching this love story unfold. I've never seen this movie before but I can tell you how it ends.

I get the girl.

And I don't just get the girl, we create a family that harbors more love than I've ever known for each other and we all live a happy and fulfilled life.

I get the whole package of what life has to offer.

The end.

Everytime I get to the end, I come back to reality and envision our whole life again and again. And I'll keep doing that until eventually every scene plays out in real life.

Today is going to be the day that I move us a step closer to that. I'm in line in the cafe to get us an iced coffee and a blueberry muffin as I wait on her when I hear a loud and familiar boom. My eyes close at the deafening sound that reverberates through my head. When I open my eyes the place is empty of the people who were here a moment ago. Except one who I notice in my peripheral. I turn my head slightly and I can't believe who it is.

November?

But not *my* November.

A glimpse is all I get before my brain throbs something fierce at the sound of another boom that sounds as if it came straight out of my own ears, and all vanished people are back, unbothered and oblivious to what I guess I was the only one to experience.

I rub my temples, easing the odd sensation as I give my order.

That odd night, it was the same thing. Whatever happened that night happened again. And the November I saw was the same one, too. It was obvious. She looked at me the same way she did before. This time, she was gone before I could even conceive of what was happening.

This is real, whatever this is. Suddenly, I'm dizzy and nauseous.

"Hey, you," November says from behind me, tapping my shoulder.

My eyes do a quick sweep of her, examining her to make sure she's really here. And really *her*. I take our tray and lead us to a booth.

"What was that for?" she snorts.

I try not to look as if something is amiss but I can't deny my swift examination isn't out of the ordinary. "Nothing. I thought you were someone else for a second."

"Oh, so you have flocks of women coming up to you like that, do you?" she jokes.

"Not flocks. They come in swarms."

"I've not seen any swarms since we met but I'll take your word for it, Prince Charming."

"They don't come around anymore. There is no competition against you."

She's speechless. I go on eating my muffin as if what I

just expressed isn't a big deal. Though we were only kidding, we know there's truth in our banter—her wondering about other women and the compliment I gave her. Now, there's only one thing to say next that makes sense.

"Will you have dinner with me tonight? I can pick you up and I'll make you something at my place."

Her big brown eyes bare into mine with a satisfied grin. "Really? You want me to have dinner with you?" she says, though with a why tone, her eyes convey something wicked and mischievous. Her foot brushes lightly against my leg, confirming my suspicion. "I'd love to."

"I LIKE YOUR PLACE. So, be honest. Did you have to clean up real quick or is it always this neat?"

"Oh, come on. Is it so surprising that a man can enjoy living in a clean space?"

"Hm...I guess it's possible," she snarks.

There isn't much to show her in my two bedroom and single bathroom house but I give her a tour anyway. "Well, as you can see, here is the living room and the kitchen."

"Has anyone ever told you that you've got a feminine touch?"

"No. I don't really have anyone over. I go out more than I ever think about having anyone here. And what's that supposed to mean, exactly? Is that a good thing?"

"Yeah, it's good! It's nice. You have more than a single lamp placed in thoughtful spaces. Was this of your own doing? Or did someone help you put this place together? Your mother? Or...an ex-girlfriend?"

I'm entertained by the concern. "Oh, no. This is all me. I went through a lamp phase. TikTok made me do it." She follows me down the hallway. "Here is the bathroom."

Her cute little nose raises, sniffing, following the scents to a candle on the counter and another one on the little table beside the toilet. "Scented candles? I'm impressed."

I smile at the silly comment. "Okay, now why would that impress you? They're just candles."

"Precisely. They're candles, not just an air freshener spray on the floor by the toilet."

My brows pinch together.

"Oh, don't look at me like that. I've known many men to have just a spray at the toilet. And other men who have nothing at all. It's a nice touch, is all."

"Wait, I'm stuck on—you said 'many men'? Uh, how–how many men...exaclty?"

She's aghast. "A woman never tells, Declan. But if you must know, not men in *that* way."

She hit my arm playfully.

"Okay, okay. Noted. But if you think you're impressed by that, watch this." I open the cabinet under the sink and pull out a wicker basket and present it to her.

"Oh! He has a candle addiction! And did TikTok make you do this, too?"

"No, I just have an addiction to candles." She laughs. "My parents got me some of these. They're my enablers. I fear I've overdone it."

She takes them one by one, smelling the collection of used and unused candles. The different aromas quickly fill the air with different smells, confusing and overwhelming my sense of smell.

"Do you want to take some?"

"What? No. I couldn't."

"Please. You'd be doing me a favor. If you don't take some then I can't get new ones. I told myself that I've got to use some up before I splurge on more. You can take the ones that haven't been lit yet. You'll really be helping me out."

She takes three unused—a forest, a cinnamon, and a marshmallow scent—and one barely used—a birthday cake scent. "I'll take these. Happy?"

"Very." I put the basket back under the sink and continue the tour. "This is my office."

Her eyes go big as they roam the office walls where my best personal and professional works are framed and proudly hung. From appealing models, male and female, posing in significant clothing and extraordinary and bizarre makeup to landscape, wildfire, stills, and street photography. "Declan," she breathes with amazement, "I had no idea!"

"No idea what?"

She picks up a pile of unframed prints on my desk. I come up from behind her, standing as close as I can without touching her. I look down at her hair, pretending I'm looking over her shoulder and getting lost in the photographs with her. "I had no idea that...that...*this* is how you see things."

I take advantage of her shuffling through my work. Discreet as I can, I watch her side profile admiring my work as I admire her. I stare as long as I can, for as long as she is distracted from where my eyes are glued. "Yeah. Pretty," I say softly. She doesn't notice that I'm talking about her.

She puts them down and wanders the office some more. I lean against the door, waiting for her to finish. "Declan, you are so talented. This is so cool. *You're* cool."

A cocky laugh comes out of him. "Okay, first you tell me that women can't get enough of me—"

"Never said that."

" —and now you can't stop telling me how amazing I am. My ego is so big right now."

She walks by me leaving the office as she grumbles something that I swear sounds like *I bet that's not all that's big.*

"What?" I ask, caught off guard and eager for her to say it again, and say it louder.

"Oh, nothing," she smirks. "And this, I assume, is your bedroom."

The door to that room is closed. I open it for her. It's awkward, at least for me. I feel like I'm presenting her my bedroom for us to make love in later, which I'm in no way planning. I wouldn't dare expect that to happen on the first time we hang out together outside of our work building. I hope she knows that.

I don't dare step inside, she does. Thankfully, her tour of my bedroom doesn't include her sitting on my bed. It would have stirred something within me that I'm not ready for. We're not in that phase yet.

I take her back to the living room and she takes a seat at the counter as I get started on our meal.

"So what's on the menu this evening, chef?"

"I'm going to make my specialty pasta—spaghetti."

She gasps. "That's my favorite! Huh, what a coincidence. Lucky me."

"Is it? That is lucky." I knew it was her favorite. I figured that if she likes it enough to add it to her Instagram bio, then it was probably good enough for me to make as the very first meal I make for her. One of many more. "Yeah, nice coincidence." I leave out the part where I pursued her Instagram.

"So what about it makes it your specialty?"

"Just the fact that I make the sauce from scratch. It's not even a family recipe or anything, it's just a simple recipe I found online." And will literally only be the second time making this recipe. The first was when I tested it out last week.

"You know what? That does make it your specialty and I'm excited to try it. Thank you for having me over and making dinner, by the way, Declan. This is really sweet."

I wink at her as I chop an onion, hoping she can't see the tears that the onion is trying to collect from my face.

This movie that I'm watching, the one we're starring in, we're at the part where we are having wine as she cooks with me, which is from her own enthusiastic insistence. We are at the part where we're having our first dinner together in the dim lighting of my thoughtfully placed lamps as she shares stories of her upbringing. My favorite story is the one where she and her friends choreographed a dance to a pop song and performed it on her friend's front yard for anyone passing by to see. It's my favorite because she cringes as she performs it for me. I cringe, too. Though it's cringier when she makes me learn it and dance it with her because if I really wanted to see the dance, then I had to do it with her, and I really wanted to see it.

It's totally worth it. That's one for the mental scrapbook.

"November, do you want to go for a little walk? I want to take you somewhere."

Her brows shoot up and her smile tells me yes before she says it. "You're just full of surprises, aren't you, Declan?" She goes to the door but I'm not yet prepared to walk out. I refill her glass of wine. "Here, you can bring this with you." She gives me a questioning glare. "There's no need to leave it behind." I wink and go to get something in my office.

I come back out with a camera, a Fujifilm xt-30.

"Oh, now I understand. Declan the photographer wants to play. Alright well, let me go check my hair."

She is about to head for the bathroom but I stop her. "No. You look..."

...like heaven would kill for your grace.

...like you don't understand how beautiful you are.

...damn near perfect.

" ...ready for the camera." I raise the camera to my eye and ask her to smile. When she does, I want to grab her soft face and pull her into mine. Instead, I snap a photo and show it to her. "See? Damn near perfect."

Her big brown eyes shoot to mine, nearly burning through my skull with something she holds back from saying, yet the smile she gives me, which is not the same sweet one she gave to the camera, tells on her. While we're playing this game of not letting our cards show all at once, I feel as if I'm peeking over at her hand and I get a glimpse of what is soon to come. Like I'm watching the behind the scenes to the making of our movie.

We walk to the grassy knoll of what I call the Kingdom of Flowers across the children's playground. When we get there the sun is low on the horizon, when the sky is at its pinkest. She watches the burning colors of the sky in awe. I capture her first impressions of my favorite place, and it makes me happy to know that she appreciates the sight as much as I do. We are right on track. The scenes are playing out in real life.

She flashes me an *I wasn't ready* glare at the sound of the clicks of the camera. "You know what? Let me be the photographer tonight." We trade the glass of wine and camera. She gushes over her first few shots. The camera displayed creamy images with subtle color of the grass, the sprinkles of color of spruce flowers and the gradient sky. "Oh my gosh, Declan, I think I'm a photographer!"

She shows me the images and I smile at her excited frenzy of eagerness. "These are great." They are awful. The compositions are all wrong, nothing is centered, and there's no proper subject, but because she took them, because they're from her point of view, her eyes, they are beyond comparison.

When the sun is completely gone we sit surrounded in the wildflowers and the weeds and crickets and butterflies as she transfers her favorite images to her phone—another awesome thing about this camera. She is having so much fun with it that I don't even care that my camera got hijacked. I got the photos I wanted anyway.

This is our first date. We don't call it that but this is what it is, isn't it? And now it's over.

I drive her home and walk her to her door and...she is playing that game that women play at the end of an evening. The keys game. She has this key ring that holds so many different kinds of cute keychains on it, slowly going through each one, giving us a bit more time. A bit more time for what? Well, that's the game, isn't it?

She waits at the door for a kiss—*the* kiss—and as much as I want to—and I want to so badly—I just can't. Not on the first date that we have yet to call a date.

In this moment I stare into her eyes to remind myself of the future we could have together if I make all the right moves. I'm going to nourish this relationship with all that I have. I want to watch it grow. Everything grows the strongest with time. I want to savor the happiness we are both feeling, the lust that is building, the butterflies that grow more and more with every smile we exchange. I want those butterflies to have a permanent residence in our hearts. So, instead, I plant a sweet and delicate one on her cheek, because we're not at that part of our movie yet.

CHAPTER 9

November

THE REV OF A LOUD ENGINE ECHOES IN THE EMPTY NIGHT OF MY street. I don't see the source of the sound right away but when it gets louder I wait and watch to see where the source is going. The source is a motorcycle. The motorcycle gets closer and closer until it stops at my house.

Eren pulls up on a jet black motorcycle—black hoodie, black gloves, black helmet—and all of a sudden I think I have a type. Especially when he gets off and starts toward me and he peels off his helmet, exposing his dark hair in perfect disarray, and stands half a foot away in front of me, forcing my head up so I can look at him.

With a large pleased grin, he says, "Surprise."

Oh, I'm surprised, alright. I can't help my own grin. Thankfully the night conceals my rosy cheeks. "I didn't know you own a motorcycle. I didn't know you ride!"

"You like?"

I cackle with amusement. "I love!"

He takes a couple steps back, openly and obviously admiring my black dress. Or my body. I really can't say. I wait for him to finish. Surprisingly, it doesn't feel as awkward as I thought it might be, and I jokingly say, "Are you done yet?"

Slowly, he closes the space between us. He places a finger, still in his glove, gently under my chin and tilts my head up. He leans down and stops right before my lips. His eyes pierce into me to see if I would stop him, to see if I want him to stop, to see if I want this moment to happen.

I do.

I gently pull on the strings of his hoodie until our lips make impact. I groan a little from the electricity. The buzz from my lips makes its way all the way down my spine. My toes curl, remembering and missing all the good parts about being with a man. My knees buckle and his arm wraps around my waist to steady me. My need for him when his lips part is undeniable. Unforgettable.

We kiss harder. Deeper. We can't keep our hands off each other. Yet, somehow I manage enough self control to pull us apart.

We can't keep from beaming. The first non-commital date is starting off strong and I am already craving to skip to the end, where we end up at his place or mine doing some unspeakable things to each other in bed. Or anywhere. Or everywhere. I'm already imagining it as I am sure he is as well. Instead, he, uh, adjusts himself and pulls out an extra helmet from his backpack, his eyes never leaving mine, handing it to me.

We put on our helmets and with a muffled voice, I ask, "How do I look?" I pose as cute as one can with a giant heavy helmet in a cute dress.

He answers, "Sexy." He takes my hand and guides me to the beefy motorcycle as if it's a horse and carriage ride and helps me on. He gets on and revs the bike a few times before turning his head as far as he can. "Hold on tight, Em."

"Go slow."

"Em, I'm not known for going slow but I'll try."

The revving drowns out my laugh as we speed off.

On the way to wherever he is taking me, when we would hit a red light or a stop sign, he would put a hand on mine, either checking to see if I'm still holding on the proper way, or maybe just to touch me. He turns his head back and asks if I'm doing okay every now and then. Every time, I tell him I'm having a good time. The last time, he patted my leg in response, pleased.

It feels very intimate, to ride a motorcycle with someone. With him. With his touching my hands and patting my leg and my arms around him and my chest against his back and my legs wide open. I feel like a completely different person. I like this person. I feel awkward coming from a long dry slumber, and I think I'm starting to see that I like Eren. Or at the very least, find him to be severely attractive. I don't know why he's never shown Liv and me this side of him before.

We arrive at a fancy bar. Not a restaurant, as I suggested we do anything but dinner. As a general rule for myself, I avoid dinner on first dates. I don't like trying to hold back on my flirty conversations while I stuff my face. Now, drinks? I could always do drinks, and at a brewery, no less.

I take off the helmet and fix my hair as best I can without a mirror. I put it in his backpack while he keeps his in his hand. "Holy shit, that was fun."

Eren gives a cocky shrug. "Yeah, I figured you'd like that."

"Why have you never told us about this?"

"I don't know. It just never came up, I guess."

I gently nudge him with my arm before looping it with his. When we enter there are tables everywhere and two more floors to explore.

"Oh wow, I love this place already."

"Wait, you've never been here?" I shake my head. "How have you been living here and not been here yet?"

"I'm sure it's been no secret that I've been something of a recluse." Since Miles, whom I'm sure Liv has had to have mentioned to him at least once or fifty times.

Understanding strikes him. "Right. Miles, that asshole."

I nod.

"Well then, allow me to show you what you've been missing out on." He goes to the bar and orders for the both of us, without asking what I want. He orders us the same drink. The bottom of the drink is a light purple and the top part looks like tea or beer.

I sip and the sweet beer dances gracefully on my tastebuds. I nod approvingly. We find a table, a booth in a lonely corner, on the second floor where it's filled with pool tables, ping pong tables, and dartboards. We sit beside each other rather than across. He looks great tonight even though all he has on is a black hoodie. But with the gloves, the helmet, the messy hair, watching him pull up on that sexy bike. It was completely unexpected, and unexpectedly and overwhelmingly alluring.

Though the bar is packed with not only adult couples and friends but families, too, it still feels very intimate with the dim lighting everywhere and nobody paying any attention to us, besides a friend group of women sitting at the bar who was eyeing Eren for a good minute when we first came upstairs.

"I've been wanting to take you out since we first met."

My heart skips even though this isn't news, thanks to Liv.

"Thank you for letting me take you out tonight"

I'm trying to get used to this. I'm not used to Eren being so blunt, even though we have skipped a few steps of what a non-date date entails and already made out, and now he can be open with his sweet talk. I also fear that I'm going to get sucked into a relationship too quickly. I remind myself that I need to recommunicate to him that I want things to stay casual. "Thanks for taking me out tonight." I open my mouth to say more but I try to craft the words sensitively.

"What's up?"

"I just want to reiterate that I'm not looking for a committed relationship. At least not right now and I don't plan on rushing this into anything more."

I can tell that he is trying to keep from revealing any reaction. He only nods.

"I wouldn't mind a casual relationship with you for as long or short as you also want, if that's all you want."

He is still nodding, deep in thought. That's not what I want. I don't want him to think too much or too hard about this. I don't want either of us to. All I want is for this casual non-date date to be fun for the both of us. Perhaps he misunderstood before. I'll show him exactly what I mean.

I take his hand and guide it underneath my dress. His eyes perk and he scoots closer to conceal what I'm making him do from anyone else. We're so close, staring intently at one another that we must look like a couple in love. No words between us, only heat. Desire. Growing hunger.

His fingers lightly trail against the fabric of my sheer lace underwear between my legs.

I repeat myself. "I said I want to keep things casual. Are you down for that? Or are you...still thinking?"

A small smirk escapes him. "I'm good with that."

Now, that's more like it.

I'm becoming breathless with his continued soft strokes, playing against me. I'm about to suggest we leave and get a room somewhere down the street when I hear Liv's voice.

"Well, it's about damn time you guys are together!"

We part like we've been caught doing something illegal

and shock hits when I see her, here. "Liv! What are you doing here?"

"I'm here with Caleb." Caleb is one of their ex-coworkers from the restaurant. "He's downstairs getting our drinks. I came up to snag us a pool table. Yeah, we didn't have anything to do since our *friends* were *busy* tonight, so we figured we'd shoot some pool for a couple hours."

Caleb walks up handing Liv her drink. "Eren! Hey! Long time no see, bud."

"Caleb, you better check if your friends are actually busy tonight or if they lied to you because they hate you." Liv looks at me when she says that last part.

"Don't listen to her, Caleb. I don't hate her. And I clearly am busy. Don't I look busy, Caleb?"

"Yes, girl, you do. Liv, you leave your sweet friend alone. She's on a date."

Ugh. Yeah. I'm not about to get into the details of this non-date date with this person I don't really know.

"And Eren," she continues, "I don't mean to bother you either, seeing as how you're also so very busy. You're both dead to me."

"I need to go to the restroom," I say suddenly, abruptly getting out of my seat. I pull Liv's hand, dragging her with me.

Once the restroom door is shut behind us Liv lets me have it. "What the fuck, dude? How come you didn't tell me you guys are dating now? You know I've been all for it! That's not fair!"

My lids press shut, not wanting to see her annoyed at me. "I know, I know. I'm sorry, but we're not dating."

She cuts me off before I can explain. "Oh, so this isn't a date? It sure looks like a date to me, and to Caleb."

"No, it's...well, he did ask me on a date but I told him that I just want a casual thing with him. So, really, we're only hanging out, not dating."

She folds her arms. "Is this your first casual hangout?"

"Yes, I swear. And we literally just got here."

She leans over a sink and huffs an annoyed breath. "I still don't understand why you didn't tell me. I mean, it's not like you have to tell me anything, but...don't we tell each other everything? Haven't we always?"

Her somber tone melts my heart. Am I being a bad friend? My eyes soften. "Awe, Liv. I didn't know that keeping this from you would make you so...gooey."

"Shut up. I just don't want it to be like last time." She's referring to when Miles tried to keep me all to himself. And for a while there, I let him. "You were the most distant you had ever been from me and it hurt and I didn't like it."

Tears fill my vision. "That won't ever happen again. I promise. This isn't going to be that. I didn't tell you about tonight because, well, I'm not used to wanting a casual relationship. I wanted to sort of get my bearings about it first. And I know you wouldn't judge me for it, especially because you're the least judgmental person I know, and you're great in that way, but I don't know, it seemed embarrassing for some reason."

"Embarrassing?" she spits. "First of all, it's only Eren. It's not like you're casual with a bunch of random strangers from dating apps." Her brows draw together. "Wait, are you? Have you been?"

"What? No."

"Okay, okay. Just wondering. I mean, even if you are, there's still nothing to judge there. Anyway, second, whoever that is out there with you is not embarrassing at all. Because that's not Eren. Who the fuck is that?" Her face contorts in bafflement.

"Right? Who is he? I don't fucking know! He showed up on a motorcycle, Liv! A fucking motorcycle!"

"Mm, mm, mm. Yummy. Who knew a little bad boy vibe on Eren could elevate his game. But when did he get a motorcycle? Has he always had one?"

"He rides for fun, not for show."

"And he broke it out because he's finally taking you on a date."

"A non-date date," I clarify. "Wait, there's more."

"More?"

"The motorcycle isn't even the craziest part." I stop breathing. I attempt to keep my face from bursting with my own disbelief.

"She stares, frozen. "Oh my god, what? Tell me."

"He basically walks over, takes off his helmet, and then we make out right in my front yard."

Liv swoons. I have never seen her swoon this hard. Sure, she thought he was cute when they first met but she clearly has an infatuation with this other Eren she walked in on tonight. To be fair, it's hard not to be. Tonight, he is giving me a little more of who he truly seems to be. Slick, dark, stylish, and...touchy. Though, I suppose I opened that door for him, and he didn't hesitate. Not for a second.

Liv pulls herself together and lets out a breath. "Okay. I wish you had warned me about how fine he is looking tonight, but that's okay. You didn't know I'd be here. I'll let that slide, I guess. And don't worry, Caleb and I won't interrupt your non-date. We're going to do our own thing and you guys can get your freak on. I was just so surprised to see you here."

"Yeah, sorry again," I wince.

"It's okay, Em. Just be safe and, you know, have fun," she winks. "And of course, tell me about it later. Or I'll beat it out of you!"

"I will."

She opens the bathroom door and pauses. She looks at me and says, "Wow. Baby's first casual relationship. I'm so proud." She wipes an imaginary tear and I go back to officially enter a new chapter of my life.

CHAPTER 10

Declan

I CHOOSE NOVEMBER. I CHOOSE HER AND ONLY HER IN THIS ENTIRE world. I'd choose her in any world, in any universe, at any point in time. Even if she doesn't choose me, my heart was claimed by her the moment those elevator doors parted and my eyes graced her charm.

It's always November in my world.

When it's Christmastime, it's November.

When it's my birthday in August, it's November.

On Easter, it's November.

November has consumed my whole consciousness.

It's always November.

I've taken her out to celebrate our three months together since dinner at my house. We didn't call it a date at the time, nor do we call any other time together a date. I don't know if she caught on to the fact that today is our three months as friends—if you look at your friends like you are in love with them—but that is what tonight is for. I don't want to make a big deal about it to her, but in my head, I'm celebrating a milestone. Also, tonight, I want to make it official. I'm going to ask her to be my girlfriend, I just need the right window.

Though the right window is surely sometime during this sunset boat ride dinner, it isn't going to be any moment during the dinner portion as she is blowing off steam about work. She's an editor for a small publishing house and there was drama about an accidental release when a book wasn't finished with its editing as well as cover art and blurb and all that. She's gone down a spiral about how the book business can be very cutthroat, which I never would have guessed. Despite being fully immersed in her ranting and venting session I'm at the same time trying to stay keen on the window just in case there is a moment of my asking her to be exclusive with me could tear down her anger and annoyance about work.

Before I knew it, we had finished our meal.

"Ugh, I'm sorry. I'm totally bringing this nice evening down."

"No, you're all good. It's okay. Really. What better way to blow off steam than on an ocean with this scenery, am I right?"

She gazes out at the setting sun. "It's beautiful."

"Come on. Let's lay out."

"Okay, I'll meet you over there. I need to grab something."

I go to the front of the boat and sprawl out. For the first

time at the sight of this miraculous world I don't have the urge to grab my camera, but revel in it and soak in the memory with nothing but my brain. Nothing but the sheer will power to forever etch this—burn this—into my mind. This view, this woman, and the moment I ask her to be mine, and I hers.

November takes her place next to me and presents me with something. It's wrapped in shiny silver wrapping paper with a gold ribbon. I look at her in awe, with gratitude, with love. She's aware after all.

"Happy three months of friendship." We both know she doesn't really mean friendship. The same way I didn't rent this boat for this friendship.

I tear the paper with eagerness to show her how excited I am about her gift, and truly, I am, even though her remembering is a gift in itself. I gasp. It's a book. On the cover is one of the photos she took of me that night. The night I took her to my Kingdom of Flowers. The first night we got to really see each other. The reason why we're here right now. The title reads *Declan: A Photographer's Eye.* I flip through the thick glossy pages of what presents everything that is in my personal online gallery. That is for the clients to get to know me better as a photographer, and now, here they are in my hands sitting in the ocean with the most beautiful woman I've ever laid my eyes on, who here she is, giving me this incredible gift.

"November," I breathe, wishing we are already exclusive so that I can kiss her. "This is so cool. I always wanted to do this for my work but I just never put in the effort. Thank you. This is...seriously...the best and most thoughtful gift I've ever received."

Her smile is brighter than the glowing sun. "I'm glad you like it."

My eyes keep glancing at her lips. I know she notices but I can't help myself to try to hide it. I have been waiting three months for this perfect moment. *The window.* "Can I–"

Before I can finish asking if I can kiss her she pounces on me with such grace that I'm surprised I didn't topple backward, but instead slowly recline us until she is lying on top of me.

This is our first kiss. Sweet. Soft. Passionate.

And it keeps going. And going. And going.

Until we're not just kissing anymore. Somehow we have fast-forwarded through this scene to the part where our bodies entangle with heat, hunger, greed, ecstasy.

This isn't part of the movie I remember watching on repeat but I will consider this to be...Let's call it a bonus feature.

"WHAT A SWEET GIFT! And, sweetie, she sounds like such a nice and lovely girl. I'm so happy for you, Deccy. I knew it would all work out."

"Thanks, mom." I don't feel like video chatting with

my mother tonight but it's the only way to stop her incessant calls. She has to hear about how the date went or she'll die. Her words, not mine. So I showed her the book November had made for me and I was going to call it quits after that but whenever we start talking I always remember how much I miss her. "How is everything at home?"

"Everything is good here. We still have our monthly cookouts with the neighbors. Oh! Tessa says hi."

Tessa always asks Mom to tell me hi. She's an ex-girlfriend from high school. They live a few houses down and her parents have grown close with my parents when we were dating. We stopped dating after graduation. It was only your typical high school puppy love. Puppy love that wouldn't have survived the real world. I wanted to be closer to a beach and she wanted to stay close to home, nowhere near a beach. Thankfully, the breakup was mutual and we could all continue to stay friendly.

"Is she back in town?"

"Well yeah, you know, she's here for Thanksgiving. That's what I call a good and loving child. I wish my own child could visit his parents for Thanksgiving," she half-jokes.

"Mom, you know the studio is booked until after the holidays. Come on."

"I know, I know. I just miss my son. My little Deccy Boy. That's not a crime!"

My mother's sweet eyes, I can't help but to say something that could cheer her up. "Buuut...maybe I can plan a visit there next year. And maybe bring November with me."

Her eyes switched from sad to overjoyed in an instant and I knew I had said the perfect thing. "Oh, Deccy! Please tell me you're serious or I will just die this very moment."

She likes to threaten with her own death. I don't know where that comes from or when she started doing that but her dramaticism is always amusing, especially when she's like that in front of people who don't know her. It distresses people sometimes. "I am. I'm serious," I laugh. "Especially now that we're, you know, official, I think I can ask her to do stuff like that with me now. I just hope that in a few months it won't feel like it's too soon to meet the parents and all that."

"Oh, you kids are too cute. I can't wait."

"Hunny, he's not a kid anymore," Dad says as he walks up behind Mom. "He's twenty-five. Come on, he doesn't want to be talked to that way, do you, Mr. Poopie Butt?"

Mom cackles at the forgotten nickname and I'm suddenly regretting planning to take November to see them. "I thought we were done with that name."

"To mom, you'll always be her little Deccy Boy. To me, you'll always be Mr. Poopie Butt."

"You guys are too funny, you know that? You know, it's not my fault that I was a baby pooping in my diaper. In fact, all babies do it. So, you're not even clever for that, Dad."

"Okay, sorry. I gotta check the stew. I'm making stew tonight. Bye, Mr. Poopie Butt."

"That's it, I'm not visiting if that's how it's going to be," I tease.

While Mom lectures Dad about this unfortunate turn of events, a loud crack sound comes from within my head. It startles me enough to drop the phone. "Holy shit," Mom hears me say.

They stop their bickering. "Deccy? Are you alright? What happened?"

"Goddamn, that was loud," I say to no one in particular.

Mom is still concerned. "What? What happened? What was loud? Can you hear me?"

"You–You didn't hear that?" When she says she didn't hear anything I know something is off. And the last time something was off...

I peek through the curtain. The moment I see a wet trail on the road, the other November comes flooding back into my memory. "Oh fu–," I stop myself from finishing that word, remembering Mom is still on the phone. "Mom, I'm going to have to call you guys back."

No response.

"Mom? Mom, are you there?"

She's gone. We're not even disconnected but I hang up anyway.

Cautiously, I open the door.

Standing there, soaked from head to toe, is her again. It's the other November. Her hair is a little more brown than black and slightly longer in length than my November's. This can't possibly be a prank. She is a completely different person. A twin? Though November doesn't have any siblings. Perhaps a long-lost twin. A long-lost family member.

Yet it still doesn't explain the way she disappeared right before my eyes.

She speaks before I do. "Here, take this." She holds out a folded piece of paper. When I don't reach for it, she repeats herself with urgency in her tone. "This is for you. I don't think I have a lot of–" She looks at her hands. " –time. Awe, shit."

Just like that, another loud cracking sound rushes to my head, but this time I don't react. Once again, I'm left confused. The nighttime sounds come back. Mr. Thompson's country music continues to blast like it was when I came home. I pick up the folded paper she dropped when she...left. I open it.

I don't know why this happens but I can assure you that it freaks me out as much as I imagine it does you. You seem to live right beside me, though not where I'm from. I have been wanting to ask, respectfully, who the hell are you? Sincerely, a distant neighbor.

CHAPTER 11

November

"Open wide," he demands.

I do as he says. What I taste is...delectable. I get some cream at the side of my mouth and wipe it away with my finger. "Oh my god, you have to try this." He gives himself a bite of my decadent chocolate cake, generous with whipped cream, and he just about dies.

"Oh shit, that's good. Trade with me." He tries to take my plate and I block him. "No way, pal. I told you that you should also get this. Didn't I say that? But nooo, you just had to have the cheesecake."

If you don't trade with me then I can't give you this." He pulls out a jewelry box from his jacket pocket. I had a feeling this was going to happen at some point. I allow my exasperation to show. "Really, Eren? A gift? A gift for what?"

He brushes off my disappointment. "Relax. It's a casual three month present. I thought women like presents."

I don't want to take it. I plead with him through my eyes to take it back and keep it out of sight.

"What, Em?" Now he's exasperated. "I can't buy you gifts? I can buy you dinners and movie tickets but I can't get you a gift? Isn't that a little silly?"

"Well, hang on. I pay for some things, too. And wouldn't it be a little contradictory of me?" I snap.

"How so?"

"It would be contradictory of me to accept that, would it not? It would contradict the point of keeping things casual if we're celebrating milestones and such, right?"

He sits slouched in his seat with his hands in his jacket pockets, sadly smirking at the red velvet box sitting on the table between us. He bites his lip, thinking. God, I don't want him to think. I like what we have. I wish he could be okay with it, too. At least for now. I mean, who knows where this thing between us will lead? I certainly have no idea. If I could choose Eren to be my one right now, I would dive in head first. I wish I would already. But something is holding me back. I don't know what but there's something in my gut that won't let me take this further. No matter how cute he is biting that lip I've enjoyed biting myself. I don't want him to be sad. I don't know if I'm going to regret being so soft but I don't want to ruin his fun when he's been so sweet about this arrangement. An agreement that mostly caters to my own wants.

I sigh. I reach across the table for it. I wait to open it in case he doesn't want to give it to me anymore, but in response, he sits up straight, bracing himself. "So…this gift means nothing more than what we already have, right?"

"Yeah. It means nothing. Promise."

He's like an excited puppy. It doesn't need to mean anything out loud but I know it means something to him. I'll be entering dangerous territory by accepting and opening this gift but I'll take his word for it.

I open the red velvet box. It is…not jewelry at all. It's a set of business cards. For my business. Stiff gold, shiny, classy, and creative. I peer at him in complete amazement. I'm in awe. The level of thoughtfulness tugs at my heart and I almost cry.

By the way he glows, he knows I don't have to say anything to express my gratitude. But this is so amazing that I can't not say anything. "Eren—"

Our waiter shows up with a to-go box and asks if we want anything else. I tell him no and we are alone again.

"That's for you."

He opens the styrofoam box and smiles.

"I ordered it when you went to the bathroom. I knew you were going to want my cake and I couldn't risk you taking mine. I love food too much. That's something you ought to know about me."

"You see? That's why I got you a gift. Because you're so—"

"Don't finish that sentence."

He considers listening, but doesn't. "You're so perfect. I admire and respect your entrepreneurship and drive for your own success. It's been awesome to sort of see it happen. It's inspiring. That's all."

I almost cry out of frustration about how I can't get myself to goddamn commit. I want to commit! I just...have this strong feeling like I'm going to be the one to mess things up, to disappoint him somehow. "Eren, I don't know how to respond to that. When you say things like that to me...I...I can't—"

"No," he cuts me off. "Please, I say it because I really want you to know. I have to tell you or I'll...I'll fucking explode. You don't need to respond to any of that. I know where you are with all this. It's okay. But just...just let me say what I need to say when I want to say them. Is that fair?"

No. It isn't fair. "I'll feel bad."

His soft groan turns mischievous. He gets out of his seat and comes up from behind me. He puts his mouth to my ear and whispers, "I only want to make you feel good." He presses his lips on my neck and helps me out of my chair and we leave the restaurant.

I'm excited that we are finally going back to my house. I've been anticipating being with him tonight but with the weather calling for rain all day, I sometimes can't help thinking about the man I keep seeing. I wonder if I stay in the rain...that maybe...

Knowing all day that it was supposed to rain tonight, I wish I had postponed our casual date. I want to test a theory and I can't do that if he's here. While I'm ready to have dirty fun with Eren, I also don't want to pass up this weather. It's been many weeks since the last time it stormed and I don't really have the patience to wait this long again.

My theory is that the rain is the doorway to this other place. The thunder and the lightning must do something that makes it so that I'm...somewhere else.

It begins to sprinkle when we make it back to my place. I would have liked to try to get out of our little social call but the whole way home he had a hand rubbing the back of my neck, massaging me and working his hand up into my hair and scratching at my scalp. Through his fingers, he was letting me know that he's eager. Ready. He'd tug my hair, similar to the way he'd pull my hair when he takes me from behind, and I was also feeling eager and ready.

I put my alternate dimension travel plans at the back of my mind. I'll deal with that later.

As soon as I open the door to my house, he bursts through and slams the door shut, immediately putting a hand behind my head and pulling me to his mouth. His tongue goes wild inside me, but gentle. He gets on his knees, slides my black silk panties to my ankles, and puts his head underneath the hem of my dress. My knees almost buckle and I lean against the door to keep me up. First, my breaths are slow and steady, my body swaying as my core tightens and releases and tightens again and again, until his fingers are in me and my legs quiver. I put my hands on his head to keep myself up. "Stop. Stop," I breathe, and moan right after.

He pulls his head out from my dress and stands up. He loses himself in my eyes as he pulls the thin straps of my dress down my shoulders and let them fall. He kisses me on each shoulder and pulls the dress down to fall and lay with my panties.

He cups one breast and squeezes around my nipple, taking it in his mouth. My hand is over his hand, the one squeezing, and my head lulls back in pure bliss. He sucks and flicks with his tongue for a few seconds before my hands begin to unbutton his shirt and pull it off his hard body. I kiss him desperately as I undo his pants. I don't even pull it all the way down. As soon as that zipper comes down I reach down into his boxers and work my hand on him.

He stops kissing me. His moans possess his whole body. His moans make me wetter. I push him onto the couch and I ride him hard and fast. He has to tell me to slow down a few times, that if I want our fun to last longer, then I need to take it down a notch because it's about to be game over.

I'm about to suggest that we have all night and we can always go again but I have a feeling there is something I have to do. I stop rolling my hips and just sit on him, letting him fondle my breasts and my hard nipples, as I try to remember what it was that I wanted to do.

Lightning flashes through the dimness of my house and sparks my memory.

The rain. Dimension traveling. When we're done here, I'll ask him to leave.

Abruptly, he flips me on my back and spreads my legs. He smiles down at me. "Em, you're soaked." He rubs a hand over me, massaging me down there, before he eats me again.

It feels so good but I want him deeper inside me. I take his head and guide him and move my hips to the strokes of his tongue. I scream out in pleasure. It doesn't matter how loud we are because by this point, the rain is falling harder and louder. I let it all out. I scream. I moan. I shout his name. "Eren! Ugh fuck me, Eren! Harder! Deeper! Faster!"

Eren is less wordy and more grunty and moany. With each grunt and moan I am ready to ride him to the end. But at least I could finish a couple times, so I don't mind letting him do what he wants. It all feels good anyway.

Finally, he is ready to explode. He turns me on my hands and knees and enters. He has one leg kneeling on the sofa and one leg standing, holding him up. One hand holds onto my hair, the other holds onto my hip to bring me back to him when I bounce off of his thrusts. With each of his thrusts he lets out grunts and I'm breathing hard and heavy. It's amazing to be loud without worry of passerby or Helena hearing. It makes all the difference in our casual hangout this evening.

When he finishes I already want to go again. He can't but he eats me out again. He trails his tongue over my body from bottom to top, licks me all over. He finishes me off with his tongue and his fingers and I come for the third time. "Fuck, that was amazing."

We're lying on the floor now. I rub his thighs, working my way to his shaft to see if he wants me. He still can't. I go down and lightly lick him. He doesn't mind that so I lick him like a lollipop. You know, casually. "So, I'm sorry to have to do this but" *lick lick lick,* "would you be mad if I asked you to leave tonight?"

He put a fallen fluffy throw pillow under his head and looks down at me. "What? Why? I thought we were having a good time. I mean..." He gestures to what I'm doing.

"Oh, don't get me wrong. This was the best fuck of my life. *You* are the best fuck of my life. But I kind of want to be alone tonight. I have some things I need to figure out for my and Liv's schedules for the week and there's some emails I've been putting off responding to that I really should finally get to."

"And you're going to do that right now?"

"Well, for the rest of the night, yeah. That's okay, right? Because...we're not..."

"Yeah. Yeah, that's totally cool with me." He gets up, gathers his clothes and goes to the bathroom.

He comes out cleaned up and dressed before I even get a single piece of clothing on. "Please don't be upset. We should never have even stayed overnight at each others' places in the first place, you know?"

"No, I understand. I'm not mad. It's fine. I'll, uh, I'll see you next time." He kisses my cheek, and when I think he's done, he's right back on my cheek and works a trail of kisses down to my neck and then back up to my cheek. He embraces my naked body but doesn't glance at it a single time before telling me goodnight.

"Thanks again for the gift," I say when he opens the door.

He nods and smiles tightly. “See ya.”

I watch him drive away then put on a pair of sweatpants and a sweater. I rummage through my desk drawers for a blank piece of paper and a pen and start writing. I fold it and put it in my raincoat pocket I throw on before braving this fucking awful weather. What a drag. Like, who actually can enjoy this? I’ll never understand.

I stand in the pouring rain between my house and my neighbor’s house for what feels like five minutes. The lightning blinks bright and angry in the dark clouds. Thunder booms but nothing else is happening. This whole thing starts to feel a bit ridiculous. A deep chuckle leaves my throat. Yes, this is silly, but I know what I experienced wasn’t in my head. “Just do it already,” I urge the powers at play.

And just like that, the sky turns white and my ears buzz until I can’t hear even that anymore. I jump at the sudden change of, well, everything and open my eyes to the neighborhood that isn’t mine. I look down the road to my left and to my right. Nobody, just like last time.

I run to the neighbor’s door and give three strong knocks. It opens within seconds.

We both know it’s happening again. And though we both sort of know what’s going on, we still have no fucking clue what’s going on. I pull the paper from my pocket. “Here. Take this.” The dumb oaf doesn’t move a muscle. “This is for you. I don’t think I have a lot of—” My fingers tingle and I assume what that could mean. “ —

time. Awe, shit." I release the paper before it can return with me.

And just like that, I'm back in the pouring rain but I'm too caught up in a discovery to be annoyed that my feet are soaking in my shoes. I realized that I felt tingles in my fingertips the first time as well. I was just too terrified and distraught to notice. But that's something. It doesn't help me to figure anything out but it's something that I know I can anticipate for next time.

I had noticed another thing.

He is extremely handsome.

This time, I find myself wanting to go back. Excited to go back. Wishing I could go back right now and that I could be there for much longer. What would it hurt if I could?

CHAPTER 12

Declan

A distant neighbor? What the hell was that supposed to mean? What was any of that perplexing letter supposed to mean? The longer I stare at the letter, the crazier I feel. It can't be real...shouldn't be real...only, it is real. I keep seeing traces of her. The proof is here in my hands but what am I to do about it?

Nothing. I can't *do anything* about this, and there's nothing *to do*. This can't be anything but a mere mistake in the universe. Or the cosmos. Or nature. All I can do is focus on what is right in front of me. On the things that are tangible and on the things that make sense, and that is November. The real November. My girlfriend, November. Not the one that materializes out of thin air from who knows where and who knows how. As far as I'm concerned, there's only her. My soulmate. *My* November.

Speaking of November, I texted her first thing this morning. I send her a cheesy morning message about how I can't wait to wrap my arms around her when I go in to work and ask if she wants to have dinner together this evening or if she is getting sick of me yet.

When I leave for work I still haven't gotten a response. It is rather unusual that she isn't even opening my texts for this long since we started texting a few months ago.

I visit her office before popping into mine. "Hey, Selena, how are you?"

"Declan! Hi, I'm good. How are you this morning?"

"Yeah, I'm good. Hey, has November come in yet?"

"No, not yet. I was going to ask you. She must be running a bit behind this morning, huh?"

"Yeah, uh, I've been texting her this morning and, uh, I haven't received anything back. She's not even opening my messages." I don't doubt that I'm pouting like a sad little puppy but I don't care. How could I have felt like I was on top of the world one day and filled with uneasiness the next?

"I just texted her, too. A few minutes ago and, uh, let me see..." She checks her phone. "Nope. Nothing. She hasn't opened my texts either. Don't worry, Declan, when she shows up I'll give her an earful for the both of us. Okay, sweetie?"

I force a friendly smile. Something doesn't feel right. Maybe it's the added oddity of the other November and her note, and it's throwing me off. Yeah, that's got to be it. I'm putting myself in a frenzy over nothing. "And don't hold back. But don't tell her I said that."

"You got it, boyfriend."

My heart leaps at the sound of that. I wonder if November has already shared the news of our official relationship status last night or if Selena is only being humorous. "Thanks, Selena. Have a good day."

When I get back to the studio I have to ask around if November has stopped by at all this morning. Karina and Dean both say they haven't seen her.

"I'm sure she'll stop by later but we're in a bit of a time crunch," Karina reminds me. "Do you think you can get your head out of the heart-shaped clouds and focus on a good photoshoot today?"

"Karina, you hurt me. You know I can do anything once I'm in the zone."

"Right. So get in the zone, my guy."

I do as she says and I'm in the zone. Our clients are an independent clothing brand that has been getting ready to launch. According to Karina, during the consultation with them, they seemed like they might be difficult to work with. They were closed off to Karina's ideas yet had no ideas of their own. Eventually, they agree to wing it. I am totally up for the challenge.

Their style is very bright, colorful, and happy. Sort of a modern vintage. The models are lively thirty-something year olds who look much younger for their ages.

They are closer in age with Karina and Dean and, me

being in my mid-twenties, some of their jokes and references in our lively conversations are lost on me but I enjoy the energy nonetheless and am grateful that they are not hard to work with after all.

I check my phone once in a blue moon and she still hasn't opened my texts. After a few hours go by, I ask Karina if she wants me to get lunch for everyone but she sees right through me and advises me to stay and be present in the job with our clients. And she's right. I've been distracted and coming off as eager to not be here or around them. I've explained to her before that it's not because I don't want to be here but that I'm excited to be around November. She expressed that she was happy to see me happy but at work, work is work.

I try to keep November out of my thoughts. We have some of their old school cartoons playing on the projector to channel the 90's. I've never seen these cartoons before. *Hey, Arnold!* is my favorite one and I ask them to keep that one playing for the rest of the shoot. The Helga character reminds me of myself, obsessed with my love, the one who I've not heard from all day so far.

A few hours later I make it through the rest of the day without checking my phone anymore or having the urge to sneak off to her office. Though I celebrate in my head, I don't feel good about it. She's ignoring me and I don't know why, especially when we had such an amazing time yesterday.

"Declan," Karina calls with a somber glare. "Selena's here to see you."

The gloss in her eyes is kind of odd but I'm just relieved to finally get an update on November because that's the only reason she has to visit me. I have to play it cool, though, because I feel like I'm quickly gaining a reputation of being lovesick.

I take my time to meet her. "Hey, Selena. What's up?"

Her eyes bare into mine, almost scared to speak. Her mouth keeps parting like she's going to say something but nothing comes out.

"What?" I flash a confused and conflicting grin. My palms start to sweat and my heart races. Each second of silence is trying to kill me. All at once, I realized that Selena has the same expression as Karina when she called me. "Are you okay? Is everything alright? Come, sit down. You look like you've seen a ghost," I say with a forced and awkward laugh. My hands and legs shake from how spooked she seems to be.

She releases a heavy breath. "Declan..."

She doesn't say anything after that for a long time and I don't chime in. I simply wait.

"Declan," she repeats, starting over. "I just got a call.

I release a breath of my own and laugh with relief. "Oh, so you finally heard from her." Selena doesn't laugh with me. "Uh, so did she tell you about yesterday? We went out for a boat ride. She loved it."

She listens as I ramble on about our perfect day. I know there's something bad she is here to say but for some reason, I can't shut my mouth to allow her to say it. When I finally do stop, she places a hand on my knee. "What? What is it? Where is she?"

"She's...in the hospital. Since last night."

"What?" I chuckle and shake my head because that can't be right. There's some mistake. "Mmm...no. I brought her home, safe and sound, last night. We went on a boat ride," I repeat, "and I brought her home right after. She was fine."

"Yes. But then she left her house sometime after that. She was heading to her friend's house."

When she doesn't continue, I say, "Okay," with a hint of impatience.

"She got in an accident."

"Oh my god." I get up. "I need to see her. What hospital is she in? Karina! I have to leave early!" As I gather my things and stuff them in my backpack, neither of them move. I figure that means it's fine that I leave. I go to them and explain anyway. "So, November's in the hospital. She got in an accident last night. I want to make sure she's alright. Maybe stop for some flowers and a Get Well bear or something. It's cool if I leave, right?"

Selena pulls me back to where we were sitting. "What hospital and what room? I need to get there before visiting hours end."

"Declan, she's—She didn't make it."

I take a moment to notice that my heart is about to beat out of my chest and calm it down. I shake my head slightly. "No."

She nods. "Yes." A tear slides down her plump cheek and

she wipes it with the back of her hand. "Her friend called the office this afternoon. She saw that I kept calling November's phone so..." she trails off. "I'm sorry. I'm so sorry. I know you liked her a lot."

Liked her? Liked *her?* I look at this woman with disgust. She's vile. I don't want to breathe the same air as her a moment longer. "Can you please...just fucking tell me...what hospital she's in."

Pain shows in her face from the sting in my tone. It hurt me, too, to see that I did that. She tells me the hospital name and I leave. I don't say thank you and I don't say sorry. I leave that nice, sweet, lovely woman with venom in her heart. I'll apologize later after I've seen the love of my life with my own eyes, alive, because this has got to be a huge mistake. She was good last night. More than good. We were happy and I brought her home unscathed. This is all a misunderstanding.

I rush through the hospital doors and try to get a visitor's pass but since I'm not considered a close friend or family member they send someone to get the family's permission. I take a seat and wait, my leg bouncing furiously. I don't know what to do with my hands. They should be doing something else, like holding her. Squeezing her hands. Running my fingers through her hair. Something other than pathetically twiddling my thumbs together or biting my fingernails. The scent of alcohol and plastic throughout the building makes me feel sick and nauseous.

Minutes later, I hear my name. "Declan? Excuse me, you're November's...new friend?"

Ouch. That hurt but not what's important right now. I push myself up from the chair using mostly my arms since my legs want to give out. "Hi. Yes."

"I'm November's friend. I'm the one..." She chokes up and fights away tears and clears her throat. "I'm the one she was going to see last night when she..." She can't speak anymore through her cries.

I hold her by the shoulders. I don't mean to but I suppose since the words of it isn't her fault wouldn't come out of my stupid mouth, my body takes over. I hope I communicated the message through my touch. Hearing her choke up makes it hard for me to get any words out. I want to tell her that I'm sorry she is sad but also that I want—need—to see her. If I can just see her with my own eyes and touch her, then maybe I can manage to get a sentence out.

She gives me a hug and I embrace her. She cries harder and her tears soak through my shirt instantly. It doesn't take long before her sobs turn into wailing.

Say something, you weak buffoon. Say something. Anything. Your girlfriend's friend is in your arms, crying. Do something. Anything.

I gently part us, creating space so I can look her in her eyes. "Hey, it'll be alright." She wipes her tears and recollects herself. "So, we've not been properly introduced. I'm Declan. And I'm sorry, I don't think I got your name."

She sniffles and wipes her nose with her shirt sleeve. “I’m November’s best friend, Liv.”

CHAPTER 13

November

This massive beast vibrates every bit of my body in the best way. The heat between my legs is like a spell that makes me forget all about my distant neighbor. I listen to the roar like it's my new favorite song. All orchestrated by this dark, delectable version of Eren.

I dressed more appropriately for it this time. Black shorts paired with a black faux leather jacket, and Doc Marten boots. I needed to match the edginess, of course.

When I come out of my daydream of what Eren swept me up for, my imagination running wild with touching, kissing, fucking, sucking, I notice that we're actually nowhere near Eren's house.

"Hey, where are we going?" I shout over the loud wooshing wind and the cars and the engine. He briefly looks back at me, his eyes glance at me through the slit of his helmet, and taps my leg in response.

We pull up to an open field filled with tents and people, vendors and games. We park and dismount the motorcycle. "Where are we?" I try not to look disappointed. I had prepared my mind and my body for a more intimate activity and the rug has been pulled out from under me when I should be getting rugburns instead.

"We're at the Hopeheart Fair." He's cocky. He can sense my sexual frustration. He knows all too well that I want him on top of me, under me, behind me, in front of me.

"But I–I thought–You said we were going to, you know, have some fun." I choose my words carefully because there's something wrong about talking in a dirty manner when I'm surrounded by families and tons of children running around.

He closes the space between us and lifts my chin. His eyes staring at me with delicate doe eyes. "Oh, we can absolutely still fuck. And we're still going to have fun. It's the fair," he says lightly. "And we'll have more fun later." He kisses my neck taking his time and nips my ear. Apparently he doesn't care about having an audience.

"Stop or I'll..."

When I never finish my thought he understands. He smirks as his eyes trail down my body, and it's like he's picturing what I couldn't finish saying. He pulls in his bottom lip with his tongue and bites it.

My breathing quickens. "Oh my gosh, let's go." I pull him along. "This is so inappropriate. Let's play your dumb fair games."

He swings an arm around me as he laughs. He's enjoying my body's reactions to him a bit too much. "I'll have you know that the Hopeheart Fair is the best fair you'll ever go to. You won't be disappointed."

"I'm already disappointed," I joke.

"Well, you won't be any more disappointed." He kisses my head.

There's an overwhelming amount of people on the fair-ground. There's so much more than what I was able to see on the way to the parking lot. Bouncy castles, game stations everywhere, food vendors, trinket vendors, a carousel, and ferris wheel, and even an outdoor movie playing where people can take a moment to relax. There's a mother breast-feeding while her other child is snacking on popcorn.

"Is this around every year?"

"Eh, they try. When they have enough money to make it as big as this, they do. But since more and more people move out of this town it's harder to keep it up every year. That's why I wanted to come. I figured since we planned on hanging out I could bring you here to experience it at least once."

"Well, this is the biggest fair I've ever—Holy shit! That's a giant panda!" We went to the booth displaying it. The line isn't long and when we are next, I go first to bounce a ping pong ball in the fake probably rigged cups. I have ten balls. Each one overshoots or bounces off the rim. I lose miserably.

Eren is determined to get me the giant panda. "How many do I need to get in to get that bear up there?"

The woman pays attention to the deep voice and recognition hits her. “Eren? From Hope Middle School?”

“Uh, yeah, I did go there.” Recognition hits him, too. “Oh, no shit. Rowan?”

“Yeah! Oh my gosh! Come here, you!” They join for a friendly hug. “Hi,” she says to me. “I’m Rowan. I used to have a huge crush on his friend when we were in middle school.”

“And then she moved away and we never saw her again. So, have you moved back? Or are you only visiting?”

“I’m only visiting. I came back, first time in a long ass time, and my aunts put me to work at this booth. That’s one way to show that I was missed, for sure.” She rolls her eyes and they land on me. “Hi again. Are you Eren’s girlfriend?”

“Hi, uh, no.” I blush. “We’re just friends. I’m Em.” I use my nickname because I would rather not go down the topic of my unique name.

She side-eyes me with an exaggerated smirk and scoffs. “Okay, girl. Whatever you say. Here he is asking how he can get this cute giant bear for you and you guys aren’t dating?” She directs that to Eren and he only shrugs in a way that says he doesn’t believe it either but it is what it is. “Okay, then. Well, the rule is, in order for you to win that bear, you need to get three balls in.” She slides the tub of balls across the table for him.

He gathers all the balls in his hands and throws them all at once.

Rowan and I stare at him with disbelief. “You moron, why did you do that?”

I think I really like Rowan.

“You just wasted your chances.”

“It worked once before. I had to try.”

She leans over the table to see if anyone saw that. It seems like no one did. “You freaking moron,” she repeats as she unties the prize from the rope. “Here you go, Em.”

“You’re just giving it to me?”

“Yes, I am. He can’t win you any giant prizes. I was embarrassed to have witnessed that. Consider it a compensation prize.”

“Awe, thanks, Rowan. You’re so sweet.”

“Yeah, thanks a lot, Rowan. I’m sure my *friend* will love to hear how you’re being mean to his friend,” Eren says with sass.

“Well, he’ll be sorry to hear that I’m happily taken now. No more swooning over him,” she gleams.

“Damn. Well, alright then. I appreciate the help.”

“Happy to help. You lovebirds have fun.”

“Oh, we–”

Eren presses on my back to move me along. “Don’t even bother. She’s just messing with you.”

We stop by a booth a few tents down for a cotton candy to share and continue to walk around. “So, who is this friend she was talking about? I’ve only ever seen you with Liv and the other restaurant people.”

"He's my childhood best friend. He doesn't live here anymore. He moved. A lot of people move out of here."

"What did your friend move for?"

"Better job opportunities."

"What sort of job opportunities?" I pull the cotton candy and let it melt in my mouth and lick my sticky fingers.

"He wanted to do film stuff. He works with a small studio. They post their work on YouTube. They do short films. He started with commercials and then wound up there."

"What about you? How come you never left?"

He shrugs and works on his own cotton candy.

"No job opportunities for you to chase?"

Another silent shrug.

"Oh, come on. If you could choose to do anything, what would it be?"

"No, seriously, I have no idea. I know it's typical for kids to grow up wanting to do a thousand things, but I never had that in me."

"Well, what are you good at?"

"I don't know. Bartending? Riding my bike? Fucking you."

"Oh, stop." I hit his arm with the back of my hand. "We've got to change that. It's such an amazing feeling to get to do what your heart is set on. We'll get you there."

"As in you and me? That sounds like a girlfriend thing to do."

It does sound like I'm crossing the line of a casual intimacy partner, but I don't want him to float in life not knowing the feeling of success. He's too good to just be a hot bartender forever.

Why can't I just commit?

As time goes on I notice that he is always at the back of my mind. He's always there, lingering, with the only thing I can imagine about him. I know what he looks like. That is all. He sits here all day, all night, in my mind, watching all that I do. Sometimes it feels like I'm never alone. Sometimes it creeps me out. Other times, well, other times I'd catch myself blushing at the memory of his face. His very handsome face.

"Em, the mean old scary rain isn't going to get you."

I turn to Liv from the chair, from looking down the street from the window instead of paying attention to our movie. I roll my eyes.

"No, seriously, what is it? What, is someone out to get you or something? You seem paranoid."

I understand. I'm irritating her. I'm not present. "If you must know," I shoot back, "it's about to storm again and I, well, I was remembering what happened a few months ago."

Her brows draw together for a long time until she

remembers. "Oh! Your...stroke. Delusion. I don't think we ever decided on what to call it. Is that what you're talking about?"

"Yeah. Just another thing to make me hate the rain." Even though as of late I've been craving it for a chance to see him again.

"I still don't understand what the other things are but sure."

"Oh, well, let me remind you." For each reason I give, I take a pillow and throw it at her for teasing. "Number one, it makes my clothes cling to my body and I hate that feeling." Throw.

"That's what umbrellas are for, darling."

I ignore her. "Number two, it makes me cold." Throw.

"It depends," she retaliates with the first pillow I threw at her, "on the weather." Pillow number two.

I catch them and reuse them as ammo. "Number three, it can get me sick." Throw. "Number four, it's loud when it pours, like it's about to real soon, and that gives me anxiety. If you've forgotten, my rain anxiety was born out of scary situations when I was little." Throw. "And now I can add the memory of having my scary little delusion in the middle of a downpour."

"Why are you attacking me?"

"You started it."

"No, you started it. Ever since you started hooking up with Eren I feel like I've had to fight for time with you, unless it's related to work."

I want to laugh but she doesn't look like she's joking. She looks embarrassed or ashamed to admit that but wants to be honest. "I'm...not used to sharing you. Not after all this time since your breakup."

Now I laugh. "That's why you're being a bully?"

"Yeah. I mean, no. You're just sitting over there sulking or whatever. What do you keep looking out the window for? We're watching a scary movie and you're barely paying attention. Are you expecting Eren or something? Is that it? You've invited him to our girls' night?"

"What, a girl can't look out her window?"

"Whatever. Just watch the damn movie."

Half an hour later I'm curled up and cuddled with her on the sofa and away from the chair, away from the window, the two of us cowering from the paranormal stuff happening to the couple in the movie. But when the woman gets pulled out of bed by an unseen entity, Liv and I go absolute batshit crazy. We scream and speak over each other, trying to get our words out of how we would shit ourselves or claims of how that wouldn't happen to us, even though we wouldn't know what we would actually do if we were really to be in that situation. The woman gets pulled out of bed and screams as it pulls her into the darkness of the hallway, slamming the door closed on her husband who woke from her screams. After the door finally opens for the husband there is lightning and thunder, and the start of an aggressive downpour ensues, and then my power goes out. We scream even louder, panic clear in our voices when we are trying to feel for our phones in the dark.

Though this time the lightning doesn't turn my vision white, I realize I need to take this opportunity to see if it will happen again. I try to head for the door unnoticed but I hear Liv's confused voice call after me when I open the door and then ignore her. If my not-neighbor has written a response to my letter, I don't want to pass up the opportunity to get it.

I stand in the street in what is almost pitch blackness. It isn't just my house that's lost power but the entire street. I hope Liv will just wait for me in the house but she comes out not long after.

"Em, what the hell?"

I sorely wish she didn't come tonight but she insisted on being here because she misses me in the way that a best friend does when she isn't giving her more attention. "I just want to be out here for a little while."

"But it's fucking freezing. Number two, remember? Now, what's going on?" she shouts through the heavily crashing rain. "You've been weird all night, so just tell me why."

I'm beginning to see that realistically, I can't keep pulling this off—running in the rain every single time without someone noticing. I really want to tell her, to explain everything from the beginning, but I'm too afraid that she won't take me seriously. I mean, who in their right mind would? "There's no—It's nothing. I'll be in in a minute."

"Are you crazy? I'm not going back in there by myself."

I turn to her, my face asking why not.

"It's dark! I'm scared! I'll just...stand here and wait with you."

A few minutes pass and nothing happens. I finally give up and we both go back inside and continue the search for our phones. We find them, both dropped on the floor, and I use the phone's flashlight to get my candlesticks out of the kitchen cabinet and spread the dim flames around the house.

We towel off and change into dry clothes. I lend Liv a set of pajamas. We sit in our silence but her stare grows loud.

"The thing I called a stroke keeps happening."

She wasn't expecting that. "Uh...please explain."

"When I called you that night and I said I saw someone in the rain, it wasn't raining there when it was raining here. I was no longer here. I was there, wherever *there* was."

Her eyes can't squint any harder, and if her brows could furrow any more together they'd become a unibrow. Her mouth contorts with hard confusion. "November, what the *fuck* did you just say? No, literally, I don't know what you just said. You might as well have been speaking a different language."

My shoulders slump as I let out a weary breath. "I don't know how else to explain it. I don't know how to say it differently. What I said is exactly how I mean it." I slump in my chair, feeling embarrassingly misunderstood. It's impossible for her to understand because what keeps happening should be impossible.

She straightens herself. “Okay, so what do you think is happening when this happens? How do you think that happens?” This is why she’s such a good friend, giving me—a crazy woman—the benefit of the doubt and hearing me out.

“I don’t know. I go *somewhere else*. Only for a few seconds, and then I always end up back in the rain.”

“Hm. Well, I don’t want to call my best friend crazy. I can’t be associated with that,” she jokes. “So, the next time you think it’s going to happen, can I be there for it?”

I want to tell her no, but what can I say if she wants to believe me? I guess it would be nice if one person believes me about this. “Uh, I guess. Though I don’t know when it will happen. I thought it might just now and it didn’t. First time, actually.” I get to thinking that maybe it didn’t happen because Liv is here.

“Just–I don’t want you to be weird again.”

“Stop calling me weird! It happened!”

“No, Em, not that. After your breakup with that loser, Miles, you were so distant. You wouldn’t tell me anything about how you were feeling, what you were going through. I was in the dark and things felt really off. I don’t want that to happen again with us. So, if you’re telling me that this... phenomenon...is real, then I’m going to believe it. Just please don’t keep me in the dark.”

As if those were the magic words, the power comes back

on. We both get spooked. “That must be the universe telling me not to. Oh, in other news, when I was at the fair with Eren—”

Liv jealously rolls her eyes at the mention of Eren.

“ —he said his childhood friend plans on visiting sometime. He’s excited for us all to hang out.”

“Oh, thank goodness. I’m tired of being a third wheel with you guys.”

CHAPTER 14

Declan

There is no hiding the bags that have grown so dark and prominent beneath my eyes. For the first few days no one would say anything but it has gotten to a point now where it could be rude to pretend like they're not there. They scream misery and you would be a shit person to ignore that, I guess is what people might have thought, because leading up to today, the funeral, the comments wouldn't stop coming.

Declan, you're not sleeping. No shit.

Declan, you need sleep. You don't say.

Declan, you poor thing. Is there anything I can do? Yeah. Bring her back. Rewind time. Change what happened.

Declan, you look like shit. You should have seen me when the love of my life was alive. I felt myself glowing.

The comments from Declan and Karina, my parents, Mr. Thompson, and others in the neighborhood and people from around the building were starting to be too much and I stopped responding. Anytime anybody would mention anything about November or the way I looked I'd become numb and silent and stare at them until they'd go away.

I can't do that today, though. Not here. Everyone here, I'm sure, feels worse than I do. There are so many people here who grew up with her, have personal stories of their own with her or about her, and have watched her grow from a baby to the awesome woman she is.

Was. Goddammit, was.

Grew into an ambitious and independent woman. Grew into a woman who had a fun sense of humor. A woman who was kind. She loved her job, loved her coworkers. And they loved her. I loved her. *I still love her.*

I'm jealous of these people who got to know her longer. It isn't fair that I was only just getting to really know her. The universe has cheated me—us—of our time together. Cheated us out of the rest of our lives together. More accurately and most importantly, stole her life.

"Good morning, everyone. For those who don't know me, I'm Liv. November was my best friend. We've been best friends since middle school. She was my first real friend. She taught me what a best friend is and what it means to be somebody's best friend. She was the best person I ever knew. Although I could talk about her for hours, I'll try to keep my deep appreciation for her short and sweet. Like she was," Liv says, bubbly. Some laughter echoes through the church.

Liv clears her throat. "Her heart was so kind. Her smile

always lit up rooms. Her voice always invited you to be open with her. Her eyes always sought to know if you were alright. Her hugs, always warm and pure." She wipes her fallen tears. "I'm going to miss those," she chokes.

She faces November now, lying there in her casket in a black dress and her hair draped over her shoulders, addressing only her. "I'm going to miss our boy talks. I'm going to miss our teasing. I'm going to miss our dumb conversations." Liv let her crying voice loose, giving up on trying to keep her composure. "I'll miss the dumb way you sing in the car, thinking you sound just like the singer until I turn the volume down on you and expose your off-key singing. I'll miss the way you have to have spaghetti once a week. I'll miss your voice at night when I need to vent to you about life. You always answered." She cries harder, no doubt at the thought that November will never answer her calls ever again. Everyone in the church is sobbing just as hard as Liv.

I'm not, and I don't know why. I loved her so much, didn't I? So, why? Why can't I produce tears that spill the way Liv's is? The heartbreak from her voice is gut-wrenching. I look around and her pain has clearly touched every single person in here. I feel like a bad boyfriend.

Oh...but I'm not her boyfriend anymore. Am I? I don't know what I am to her now and suddenly I feel out of place.

"November, girl, you were a beautiful soul. I never would have gotten this far in life without your constant love and support and motivation and pushing me to go further than I ever believed I could go. Because of you, I get to say that I know what pure love is, what a real friend is, what a true bond is. I am honored to have been your best friend and I hope I came close to being that for you, November." She goes to the casket and gives her a long kiss on the forehead.

November's mother and step-father, who I met in the hospital, embrace Liv for a long time, the three of them sharing the pain of knowing and loving November so intimately and having lost her.

It feels like just yesterday I was standing in an elevator with her and now, here I stand, invited up here by Liv and her family to give a eulogy. "He–Hello, everyone. Uh, my name is Declan." I grip the podium tight with my sweaty palms. "I have only known November for three months when I asked her to be my girlfriend." *Oh god, did that sound juvenile? Should I have said exclusive instead? I'm overthinking, I think. Forget it. Keep going.* "Uh, she..." I pry my eyes away from all these strangers. But when my eyes land upon her...

"Man, she's beautiful," I unintentionally breathe into the mic. I shake my head. I can't start spewing all the flowery things I wish I could keep saying to her. "You know, we met in an elevator." I smile at the memory. "Yeah, her ringtone was music from an old YouTube channel I used to love. I don't know anyone who watched this creator like I used to, and still do. Also, she was the only one I knew to have a personalized ringtone. Like, I thought nobody does that anymore." There's light laughter from the pews. "That got my attention. I had spilled coffee on my shirt that morning and she told me she liked my shirt anyway." I replay that moment a few times, watching it very closely, never wanting it to end. I chortle, remembering how crossing paths with her caused me to forget where I was going. "I thought she had to be flirting with me."

More light laughter.

"I'm sure she wasn't at the time. She was only being friendly." A lump forms in my throat. "That was the thing about her, as I'm sure you all already know, that she was simply nice. Always. To everyone. She was sweet. She was smart. Funny as hell. Sorry, Father." Some people found that funny, some not so much.

I am remembering her in the way that I had met her and in the way that we were becoming friends. It's heavy. "I'll miss our lunch dates at work. I'll miss her ordering for me after she noticed I always ordered the same thing.

"I'd always want the same thing, but she would always tell me 'Live! Live through this menu, Declan! Explore!' On our first date, I brought her to my house and I made her dinner. After dinner, I took her to my favorite spot in my neighborhood. We talked for a long time there. We talked about what we wanted for ourselves in the future. I said I hoped I'd see her in mine. And she said 'Declan, I like you a lot. In my future, I just want to see you happy.' And I sat there just letting that sink in. While I was thinking about me, she was also thinking about me." I turn to her. "November, you are the most genuine and selfless person

I've ever had the pleasure of knowing. And I will still be seeing you in my future, because I will *never* forget you."

I can't say how much longer the funeral goes on for but it's dark when I notice I'm back home and drinking my third beer. The thunder wakes me from a fugue state and triggers the other November to enter my thoughts. So now I'm thinking about her and the first time I saw her. And the time I thought I saw her in the cafe. Yes, it's all coming back to me now, very distinctly. And then some time ago when she—

Oh fuck. The note. My heart tugs at the thought that I might be able to speak to her again. At some point. Maybe. Unless that phenomenon ended with my November. Either way, the notion stirs the numbness and the alcohol away and I become eager to get my words out. I don't know what words yet but something has to come out, has to be expressed. It has been over a week since I last spoke to her. I'm desperate to feel like I still have her.

I don't know how long I've been writing at my desk in the office, the one November loved so much, and I don't even notice when it starts raining. All I am is lost in words for my November.

part two

CHAPTER 15

Declan

GUILT WAS A NEW FEELING THAT'S BEEN CULTIVATING. OVER TIME, I had begun to blame myself for her accident. If not for me, she never would have been at the wrong place at the wrong time. Guilt gnaws at my senses so much that I couldn't stop texting Liv for a whole week apologizing for my part in her best friend's death and asking if she and her family hate me or if they can forgive me, but as it turned out, Liv also harbors some guilt of her own. If not for November wanting to go to her house to talk about her new boyfriend.

She cried about how she was supposed to drive to November's place instead, but she was feeling lazy. *Can you believe that? Because I was too lazy.* She felt silly the first time she expressed that to me, which was also the first time she shared that with someone. Maybe also her only time. It didn't seem like she could admit that out loud again.

I felt bad that I felt a tiny bit of solace, that I wasn't the only one to feel at fault. And I felt guilty to have felt some weight off my shoulders. I want to feel it all, though. Every last ounce. It's the least I can do, right? To feel bad?

I no longer know how to function. We didn't know each other very long, yet I feel so deeply for her. I'm confused on where I stand in her death and about how deeply this should be affecting me. I'd known her for three months and I was already planning a future with her. Now that she's gone I can see clearly now how fast I was moving us in my mind.

But you can't help who you love. If it was up to me, I'd have taken it much slower, but you also can't control passion. And though I didn't know her long, it felt as if I'd known her for years. And though I've gained clarity on how fast my feelings for her grew, my heart still aches for her. It aches in her absence, no matter how I spin it to myself that this level of pain doesn't make sense.

I believed we were soulmates. I felt it. I still feel it. We were meant to be together forever. But what do you do when your forever person is gone before your life with them even begins? We were robbed.

It's nearly noon and I'm still in bed. The hangover won't go away any faster by staying in bed. Every toss and turn feels like I'm going to fall off the earth. I need this pity party to stop and force myself to do something productive today. I also need food in my stomach.

Heavy winds rustle the leaves loudly about, the sun

nowhere to be seen. This is good. My perfect weather. *November.*

The thought of her makes me want to go back to bed but I fight the urge. I sit on my porch with a cup of coffee and a burnt buttered toast.

Mr. Thompson is leaving his house when he sees me. “Hey, kid!” Ah, he likes me today. “How are you doing today? Oh, still in your jammies, huh? Long night? Partying?”

A flash of my “long night” drinking alone looking at photos of us, aching for her voice and her smell and her touch permeates my senses and I shut my eyes to make it go away. “Something like that. What are you up to today, Mr. Thompson?”

“I’m going to pick up my niece. We’re going to spend the day together.”

“That sounds nice.”

“Yes. She’s a very good girl, my niece. She’s the sweetest kid. You’d love her.”

“Well, I hope to meet her sometime.”

“You may meet her today. I’m bringing her here and we’re going to see if we can recreate my late wife’s special cookie recipe. I’ve been craving those dang things but I can never get the recipe right. My niece, though, she’s become quite the baker. Yup. She’s a special girl. She’s got that same spark, that same kind of passion that it takes to bake the perfect cookie. Just like my wife.”

“Awe, that’s beautiful, Mr. Thompson. That warms my heart to hear that. I know she’ll get it just right.”

He goes to his car and opens the door, but before getting in, he says, "Son, are you alright?"

He is chatty today. I've never gotten this much wholesome interaction from him before. His simple question breaks me and I don't want to speak for fear that my voice will croak and open the floodgates. So I nod. He can't see the tears welling, or maybe he can, I don't know, but they build until it covers the whole of my vision, falling only when I blink. I'm grateful that the chill in the air dries the wet streaks down my cheeks instantaneously.

Mr. Thompson tilts his head down momentarily and looks back up at me and nods back. He gets in his car and drives away.

I dress for the day and want to take a walk to the Kingdom of Flowers. I stuff my backpack with a thermos of hot cocoa, a couple of meat and cheese snacks, and the book she had made for me. I throw on my noise cancelling headphones and trek through the falling leaves as songs of love and heartbreak play at random, each song an attack on my heart.

When I make it to the Kingdom I get comfortable underneath the spruce flower tree, resting my back against the trunk as I unpack the thermos and the book. The hot chocolate sends shivers down my spine, it makes the hairs on my arms stand. I have combed through this book about a hundred times now, automatically skipping to my favorite image. The reason why I wanted to bring the book with me in the first place. The photo of us. I'm so thankful that she overtook the camera that night, or else this selfie of us wouldn't exist.

The only photo I have where the two of us look like a real couple, because we thought we'd have more time.

I study her face. The sharp curve of her jaw, the openness of her big smile, the joy in her eyes, the faded color of her red lipstick, the thickness of her brows, the beauty mark on her cheek, and her dark brown hair.

I take off my headphones. It's quiet, yet loud with the world. I haven't heard the birds' choir since she'd gone. I haven't heard the tall grass gently collide against each other. Haven't noticed the scent of dying leaves, haven't realized the cars roaring by or the chatter around me. Haven't noticed the change all around me. I didn't notice that autumn had come.

It's always November in my world, I remember telling myself.

The only thing I seemed to have noticed was how dull and drab the world suddenly looked, like her light outshone the sun, the stars, the moon. Like when she left this world, all light expired with her.

"You're beautiful," I say to her image. "This is still our story, it just looks different now. It's still you and me, but you've got to wait for me to catch up to you. In the meantime, the rest of my story will be a plot twist. I have no idea what this new story will entail. I try to see what could be ahead, and just like before I met you, I see nothing. I don't see a future. When I met you, I saw *everything*. Now, it's like my mind has run out of film and I can only take polaroids. I can only take in the moments as they come."

I put my hands over my face wanting to suppress that way of thinking. It all feels delusional now. My life had quickly become a whole production, a whole song and dance. Now, it's a dark and empty theater.

For another half hour I laid here listening to songs that felt like soundtracks to our love, imagining that she was lying here with me. I will it so strongly that when I close my eyes I think of her hand in mine. Desperately, I turn my head and open my eyes wanting to see her sweet face, stealing my breath, something only she could do.

When it's Christmas, it's November. I wish I could have Christmas with you.

When it's the new year, it's November. And I gently lift your head by your chin, draw you in, and kiss you at the stroke of midnight.

When it's Valentine's Day, it's November. February is all about my love for you.

I chuckle at a gift idea I just thought of. I'd have made a calendar where every month is November. She would have loved that. I cover my face, smiling, playing the scenario out in my head but wanting to hide the fact that I'm laughing by myself in case anyone else is around.

At the drop of a tear sliding down the side of my face I know it's time to go home. And I think of her all the way home, too, urging for this grief to subside.

Mr. Thompson returns home at the same time I am. He

quickly gets out of the car to greet me again. "Declan!" He waves. "Perfect timing! I want you to meet my niece." No one comes out of the car. "Oh come on, don't be shy," he says to the passenger.

As the passenger door opens, he says, "This is my brilliant niece, Mia."

Long legs covered in stockings slide out. Not at all what I was expecting. The long legs pull out a woman who has to be at least a year or two younger than me. Blonde hair, slim figure, and makeup done nicely in a way that looks natural. Honestly, they could tell me that she's a professional model and I would believe them. "Hi, Declan," she says shyly once she's fully out.

Immediately, I'm so drawn to her. I float over with a hand out. "Hi, Mia. Nice to meet you. I–I was expecting a little girl from the way Mr. Thompson talked about you, to be honest."

Her eyes roll to her uncle behind the car now, but he was no longer paying attention to us. "Yeah, he still thinks of me as a little girl. It's sweet but it'll confuse people, for sure."

We stand with awkward smiles when we finally realize that Mr.Thompson is trying to carry all his grocery bags at once. "Shit, let me get those," I rush.

He gladly lets me take them all off his hands. He closes the trunk and hurries to unlock the front door.

He must have at least twenty keys to fiddle with. The bags start to get heavy but I dare not show it. "Maybe you should mark the house key, huh?" I joke.

He scoffs. "Son, I know the key by heart. It's the key to my home, you know?"

He tries three more keys before finding the one that works.

Mia gestures for me to go in first. "You don't need to pretend they're not heavy. I know what we got," she laughs.

"Feels like bricks." I rush inside and place them on the kitchen floor.

"Thanks for the help, son. I'll be right back."

He disappears behind a wall that I can't see beyond and hear a door close.

Mia begins to put the groceries away and I don't know what to do, if I should stay or help or leave. I stand dumbly with my hands in my pockets. "I thought you were only staying for the day."

"I am."

I eye the groceries, confused. "Oh."

She giggles and explains. "He always takes me with him to get groceries. I guess maybe he likes the company when he needs to restock. He talks my ears off the whole time. I enjoy it. He's funny."

My eyes shoot open as if to say *Come again?* "I'm sorry, I thought you said that Mr. Thompson is funny."

"He is. Do you not know that he used to be a stand up comedian?"

"Shut up," I accidentally blurt.

"You don't know this? How do you live next door to a legend and not know? In all fairness, that was a very long time ago. He started after high school and stopped in his thirties, when Aunt Helena passed away. He's never gone back to doing it since."

"Oh, my god." It suddenly occurs to me that that may be why he gets so cranky sometimes. It also suddenly occurs to me that I've never wondered about might have happened with his wife.

"He was good. I've seen tapes. It never went anywhere except around here but I've always thought that it could if he never gave it up. There were so many nights where he'd pack the establishments he'd perform at. He was something of a local legend back in the day."

I run a hand through my hair. "I never would have guessed. I've never heard him say a single funny thing since I moved here."

"Yeah well, that'll happen when you lose the love of your life."

I understand that sentiment all too well, but I can't imagine it to his extent.

Mia's on her tippy toes, reaching for the top of a cabinet for a recipe book.

"I got you." I reach for the book and hold it out for her to take it, and I notice the gap between us has mostly closed. Her body is so close now that I can feel the heat of her breath on my face.

"Thanks," she says softly, as if telling me a secret.

She bares into my eyes, stealing glances at my lips, and the hair that falls loosely over my forehead. "I–Sorry, I have to go." I grab my bag and take brisk steps for the door.

"Declan, I'm sorry," she calls. "I thought—"

"No, you didn't do anything," I say. I forgot I have a...a thing I need to do. Have fun baking and nice meeting you, Mia."

I feel bad for walking out in a rush like that, but I could tell that if I didn't leave, a new story would begin and I'm not ready for the tale of November to end. Ours is a short film that I haven't digested yet.

With Mia, who knows? It could be a horror or a whole goddamn fantasy trilogy for all I know. Just the thought of it is too much to handle.

CHAPTER 16

November

Waiting to see my distant neighbor is becoming brutal. Rain brings me automatic anticipation now, and tonight, the anticipation is strong. I've told Liv and Eren that I would meet them at the bar, where we'll be meeting Eren's mystery childhood friend for the first time.

I told them I have a meeting. Technically, I'm not lying. I am waiting to meet with someone, just not for work or with anyone in this apparent universe. Liv asked if she needs to be present for it and I told her it's more for personal touches, which led her to believe it's related to the art.

I watch the sun start to disappear behind the houses across the street as I sit on my porch watching the storm roll in.

It rolls in fast. My fingertips feel like static and I take a few deep breaths. A flash of white overwhelms my vision, this time there is no sound that comes with it, and once again, I enter a neighborhood that isn't my neighborhood. I snap upright and rush to the next house. Again, he's not outside, so I knock on the door.

It opens slowly. I don't blabber like last time. I give him the opportunity to have the first word.

"November," he breathes. He studies my face, my clothes all the way down to my shoes. He takes the ends of my hair and inspects it. "Your hair. It's different," he says sadly, and then attempts a smile. "It looks good."

He's drunk.

"It looks great. You look great."

My face grows hot and I want to shrink away because I know I don't look great at all. I'm wearing sweats, a stained shirt from spilling coffee this morning, and I'm wearing zero makeup. I clear my throat. "D-Did you read my letter?"

"Letter?" His mind goes somewhere, like he's trudging through his consciousness for the letter, and on the way, runs into something he doesn't want to see. Then his eyes spark. He must have found it. "Ah, yes. That odd letter you gave me. I wrote you one back." He runs to fetch it and is back a moment later.

I hold out my hand, eager to read his response. He must have had so many questions like I did, like I still do.

"Uh uh. I'll give it to you at our spot." He smiles through sadness again with forced delight. He gently, slowly, sweetly slides his fingers in mine. I'm mesmerized by his fluidity, his fluidity, his movements, his calm voice. He's acting like he knows me, like we're old friends. Or old lovers.

Hand in hand we walk down the desolate street. My heart pounds so strongly that I'm wanting to disappear before him, but it's not happening. This visit is different. Not only is it lasting longer but…I think he's making it so, somehow. If I had to guess, there is something about him that is keeping me here. Obviously I can't know that for sure and there is no way to know for sure. All I have is a hunch, a hunch coursing through my body.

"I know this place," I say.

"Of course you do. It's the Kingdom. Our Kingdom. Our Kingdom of Flowers."

I don't know what is so "of course" about it but I ignore that. "I love coming here, though there's more flowers here than the one I visit."

His smile is tight. "It's spruce, but there's some life. And I know you love coming here, silly."

I don't ask why he thinks that. I just want to keep him looking at me the way that he is. Keep brushing against my arm like he is. Keep saying these flowery things that make my heart skip. I don't want to break this spell.

I lie down in the soft, dry grass. In the bloom. With the butterflies. A moment later he stands over me, hands in his pockets and his long wavy hair hanging down his face as he looks down at me. He sits beside me, knees up. I sit up and now we're facing each other. His tight smile never falters, perhaps softened a little. He looks like he's holding himself back from me, a stark difference from our previous encounters. "Who are you?"

He looks down shyly, then back up at me. “November. You know.”

I shake my head subtly. “I’ve...never seen you in my life. Not before whatever this is began.”

He notices the coffee stain on my shirt. “You know...the best thing I ever did was spill coffee on myself that day.”

I want to know what that means but don’t say anything.

He throws a leg around me and puts his hands around me and pulls me into him, between each other’s legs, our faces inches apart.

“I...don’t know what I’m doing here,” I tell him softly, confused.

“You know what I did today? I begged the universe or God or whatever higher power there is to see you in my dreams just so we can talk one last time. For a proper goodbye.”

The pain in his voice, his words, his eyes...it makes me want to cry.

“November...am I dreaming?”

I don’t respond. I don’t understand what’s happening but I want to see where this goes.

He presses his lips on my knuckles as a tear falls. “Please tell me I’m not dreaming. Please tell me your death is the dream. A nightmare. Please.”

He waits for me to answer, begs through his stare for me to tell him what he wants to hear, and all at once, I understand a little bit. A tear runs down my cheek. “I–” I stammer. “I’m not...her.”

"Don't—" he says as he quickly turns from me, pained.

Tears fall freely down my face now. "I'm sorry."

"November, don't–don't say that."

I take notice that he only says my whole name. I'm used to most people calling me Em. I hold on to his voice saying my name. I like hearing him say it.

"Okay? You–You're confused. I can see that. But you're November. My November. You'll remember soon enough." His fingers tuck my hair behind an ear and trails a finger down my face, guiding me by the chin to close the space between us.

When our lips touch I think for sure I'll be gone. To my surprise, when we pull back and he is still sitting in front of me, I go in for another kiss.

Seconds later I am back in my reality, still on my porch. I must have looked like I was staring into space. Farther than space. Through the entire universe.

I touch my lips, the remnants of him still there. The feeling of his tongue still there.

Goosebumps envelope my entire body and I go inside. I close my sweater tighter when I feel something in my pocket. I pull out a folded paper. He must have snuck it in.

November,

It's you. It will always be you. When it's Christmas, it's November. When it's springtime, it's November. In May, June, or July, it's November. It's always November. You consume my mind, my heart, and my soul in this universe and any other. I'll love you anywhere, all the time, and always.

Forever yours,

Your distant neighbor, Declan.

"I'm sorry, Eren."

"No, it's okay. Obviously I don't want you to force yourself to come if you're not feeling well. I can come over if you want. Just me, and take care of my girl."

"See, this is where being casual comes perfectly into play. You don't have to feel obligated to miss out on hanging out with your friend to take care of me. There's no ties here. You're all good and I'll be okay. It's just a tiny cold, anyway."

I hear Liv asking him what's holding me and him informing her that I won't be there. I can hear her say something about dragging my ass out of the house and something about killing me.

"They said they understand," Eren says.

I roll my eyes at the lie. "Maybe tomorrow? Or the next day? We'll see how I feel. I'm sorry again. I'll make it up to you. Not Liv, though, that unsympathetic witch."

He laughs. He has a nice laugh. It's low and deep and cute. "Alright well, I'll let you get your rest, then. Let me know if you need anything, okay? Like, anything and I'll come running."

"Thanks, Eren."

"That includes a midnight booty call. Sick or not. If you're down, I'm down."

The more he makes me smile, the worse I feel about thinking about Declan. I'm giddy about finally having a name to go with the face. His phantom lips linger on my lips all these hours later and I can't help but think about it. We had such a long amount of time together. At least it felt like a long time, yet I was only "gone" for a minute or so. "I'll certainly let you know. Now, quit worrying about me and go have fun."

"Alright. I'll call you later, sexy."

A tinge of guilt creeps up. Why do I feel like I'm doing something wrong? I'm not cheating on a boyfriend because I don't have a boyfriend. Would it be cheating if the other man doesn't exist? Or...does exist but...not here?

I shake my head and erase the thoughts. This is a non-issue. I lie in bed and barely hear the dark, bad weather as I think about Declan.

All I do for the rest of the evening is relive his green eyes on me and re-read his note. His words are like poetry. His whole being is that of a romantic poet. It's captivating and I want more of that—more of him. His looking at me, his wanting me, his hand through my hair, his puppy love eyes.

My hands shake with an aching and a longing to be with him again. I feel like a drug addict going through a withdrawal. I really am starting to feel sick. I cling onto his words like medicine.

—in this universe and any other.

It's always November.

CHAPTER 17

Declan

It's been a long time since I've seen her face, heard her voice...touched her warm body. I have questioned how much I drank last night to have had such a vivid...experience. I decide it's real, that she really came to me and gave me what I wished for, to see her and talk to her one last time. I didn't say goodbye, though. I didn't want to. I couldn't. How could I ruin such a moment with such a lasting and final word?

She didn't remember me but maybe sometimes the dead can't remember. Maybe it was never another November but a warning spirit, a foreshadowing spirit, this whole time. The universe knew her time was coming and I couldn't interpret its warning. I don't know how the note, nor signing the note as my distant neighbor, fit into this conclusion, not yet.

At work, we're wrapping up a shoot for a group of ballerina dancers and they have given us free tickets for any one of their Christmas shows next month. One ticket for each of us and one for our plus ones. From my peripheral view, I notice they share a look that I'm sure communicates something that has to do with me. I have a feeling I know what that's about.

Dean walks over, slapping a hand on my back. "So this is pretty awesome, right? Finally, something to give us an excuse to hang out again."

"Yeah, it sounds fun."

"Do you plan on going?"

"Yeah, maybe. We'll see."

I feel their shared look even though it's quick and could easily be missed if you aren't paying attention, but I'm paying attention. There's an odd energy in the air and something is brewing.

"Yeah, I'll have to talk with the wife, make sure she keeps some time open for us to go. I've never cared for ballet but it'll be the perfect date night." He hesitates to say more.

"Did someone say date night?" Karina chimes. "That sounds great. I was already thinking about bringing a girlfriend but we should do a triple date! That'll be fun, right?"

My eyes roll away from them, knowing exactly where this is leading. "Oh yeah, perfect. Oh but wait, Declan doesn't have a date," I mimic Karina's voice. "How ever shall we fix this? Oh I know! How about we set him up with someone? And then maybe he'll stop moping about."

They've been caught. "What? No," Karina stammers.

"We weren't thinking that, smarty pants, but now that you said something—you, not me—that girlfriend I was thinking about taking—"

"Bullshit," I interject.

" —well, she's suddenly free for someone else to take her."

"Sorry, Karina, but that's not going to happen."

"Why the hell not? And please, and I mean no offense by this, don't say it's because you're still hung up on November. I mean, again, no offense, but you only knew her for three months. You've got to be over it by now, right?"

Dean winces.

I scoff, annoyed. "Wow. You've got some fucking nerve, huh?" I jam my things in my backpack and start to leave.

"Okay, I'm sorry! That was insensitive, but...I mean, someone's got to tell you," she eyed Dean, annoyed herself, "that is...kind of...odd. No? How it's...it's been a couple months since her passing and you're still stuck on her, someone you barely knew."

I know the odd truth of this. I realized this myself not that long ago, but a sudden death is no small thing. "Pain is pain and I don't know how else to handle it. Someone lost her *life*. Someone I was growing close to. Sure, I didn't know everything about her but I was prepared to. I was going to. I wanted to. And we never got there. We can't, because she *died*. She's *dead* now, Karina, do you get that? Or has that never happened to you?"

I storm out before another word from anyone is said. I can't believe her audacity!

On my way home, as I have some time to calm down, I reconsider the fact that I do need to move on. I'm well aware that I can't keep wallowing for a woman who is no longer on this earth.

Even though she exists someplace else, it seems.

I shake this thought away and force myself back into reality. I may have been a bit harsh toward Karina. I get home, open a beer, then text her that I'm sorry for snapping at her and that I don't need to be set up with anyone because...I have in fact already moved on and will be asking her to be my plus one.

I lie. I don't want to be set up and this is the only thing I can come up with to keep it from happening.

She responds, saying that I have nothing to be sorry for and that she is the one who is sorry, and that she just wants me to be okay, and that she is very curious to know who the lucky woman is.

I am also curious to know who this plus one is going to end up being.

There's a knock on the door. For a heartbeat I think it's going to be her, but that only comes with an explosive sound, but I also wasn't expecting to see—

"Mia," I say, surprised.

"Hi," she says nervously.

"Hey. What's up? Is everything alright?"

"Oh yeah, everything is great. My uncle wants me to

invite you over to try out my new batch. He thinks we got it down perfectly this time, even though I think it tastes like the last batch."

"Oh uh..."

She notices the beer in my hand. "If I'm interrupting something..."

"No, no. I'll come over. Uh, just one sec." I run to the fridge and grab another beer. I hold it out for her.

"Oh thanks," she says cheerfully.

At the sound of us entering the house, we hear Mr. Thompson run away to his room. "Uh, Uncle?" She knocks on his door. "Uncle, we'll wait for you."

I hear a muffled, "Go ahead. I'm going to be on the phone for a while with your mother." Followed was an immediate quiet and disappointed grunt.

"Okay, so I think it's just you and me for now. He's on the phone with my mother."

I follow her to the dining table and she unclothes a basket of freshly baked cookies. We clinked beers and take a bite at the same time.

My brows rise from the lightness from such a delectable and decadent sweet treat. I don't have a big sweet tooth but this is a perfect cookie, to my own personal taste buds.

"Do you like it?"

"Are you kidding? This is the best cookie I've ever had! Your aunt created the perfect cookie recipe. I think you knocked it out of the park. There's no way it could be any better than this."

Her cheeks turn a light pink. “Thanks, Declan. Uncle wants to take it over to my mother. That’s probably what they’re talking about right now. They’ve missed her cookies over the years and now everyone will be happy to know that I can recreate it.”

“That’s awesome. Let’s cheers to that.” We clink beers again and drink.

“So what do you do?”

“I’m a photographer. How about you?”

“I’m a baker for a local family-owned bakery.”

“Ah, that sounds like it suits you.”

“It does. They’re great.”

Silence. I can hear my breathing in the dead quiet.

She keeps turning around to see if Mr. Thompson is coming back. “Sorry about my uncle calling you over and then disappearing. Again.” She chuckles awkwardly.

“Not a problem. In fact, I didn’t know he was fond of me in any way.”

“Why? What do you mean?”

“I’m always the first to exchange greetings when it comes to him. Oh, I almost ran him over once. I thought for sure he hated me if he didn’t already.”

“Well, he must like you very much to have you over for a second time, and to share his wife’s cookies, no less.”

“Inviting me over and then disappearing is liking me very much?”

“For a person like him? That’s practically a hug.”

I pretend to dust my shoulder off. "I guess I've always known how charming I am."

Through a smile, she says, "On a serious note, you are quite charming." She avoids eye contact when she says it. "And...I'm sorry if I made you uncomfortable the other day. I...misread the vibe."

I'm stuck on how she thinks I'm charming. She drops the bait right in my lap. People want me to move on, fine. I'll let them think I've moved on. "Mia, do you like ballet?"

CHAPTER 18

November

THE CLOSEST THING TO POETRY THAT HE EXPRESSES ARE THE varying ways he tells me he can't wait to undress me. Whenever he does, glimpses of Declan peeks through my mind.

Is it considered cheating to be thinking of another man from another world during? Even though we're not dating?

Always, since the beginning, yes, glimpses of my distant neighbor are there, lurking, but if there is one thing to be said about Eren, it would be that when it comes to the bedroom, he always demands my attention back to him without knowing he even needed to. His body has become hard. He calls it the girlfriend effect and then, of course, I have to remind him that we aren't dating. He'll then double down on the sentiment still holding true. He looked great before, but this new body is certainly appreciated.

He wants to *demonstrate* his poetry before Liv arrives but

that will only leave us five to ten minutes and I'm not willing to chance it.

Liv is super excited for me to meet this mystery friend. That's how they refer to him when they talk with me about him since I haven't met him yet and he's been here all week. And this mystery friend has taken a liking to Liv and she to him, which honestly was surprisingly to learn because she had sworn off relationships since her last controlling ex. Before that deadbeat there was a high school sweetheart who she dated all of high school. He broke up with her because he wanted them to explore their options. At the same time, we both hated him for that reason, though she tried to play it cool.

Now that we're fully grown adults we understand where he was coming from and that turned out to be the right choice because they did want different things. He wanted a more traditional life and she wasn't even sure if she was going to want kids in her twenties. Seeing his posts on Facebook over the years, he got what he wanted. He met someone in his first year of college and they got married and now they have two small children.

Liv, on the other hand, likes a man who knows how to have a silly goose time. Apparently, that would be Eren's friend. What could have possibly happened in the few days she'd known him to make her so giddy? My mind is too focused on Declan that I haven't been paying close attention to how infatuated she's become with this man. I'm ready to see it tonight, though.

"You should see them together," Eren says. "It's gross. I'm sad that my boy will be leaving tomorrow but at least I won't have to see them flirting anymore. My god, is that what we look like to her?" He laughs. "You're lucky you've been sick all week and didn't have to witness such annoying behavior," he teases.

"You're overreacting."

"No, Em, I'm not. Liv turns him into some creature I don't recognize."

Whenever he calls me Em I think about how Declan always calls me November and I play his voice saying my name on repeat in my head, zoning out.

There's a knock on the door. I roll my eyes at Eren and open it.

"Finally!" Liv hugs me tightly, pushing me backward. "I'm so glad you made it or you'll have missed out on literally the sexiest man alive."

Eren clears his throat and lifts his shirt to reveal his new abs.

Liv ignores him but I admire it.

"Ugh! He's so sweet, too. Sensitive, at least with me."

Eren gags. "Of course he would be. You're a girl."

"I'm a woman," she spits back. "He's just so..." she sighs, melting into the couch.

"See what I mean, Em? Annoying."

"Is he almost here?" I ask.

Eren checks for a text from him but Liv is the one with

the update. "He said he'll be here in about a couple minutes."

"Wow, I'm just chopped liver then, huh?"

"You guys are ridiculous," I say as I shake my head at them both.

"He said he can't wait to meet you," Liv says.

"Me? Why me?"

"Oh, well...because..." she tries to eye Eren discreetly. I guess that was supposed to mean that he can't wait to meet the woman his best friend is so hung up on, has been so hung up on. "Because you're my best friend and I always speak so highly of you. That's all."

"Uh huh." I doubt she's uttered more than a sentence about me, and the one sentence was probably about how I was unwell the night I was supposed to meet him for the first time. After that, I was probably also chopped liver.

For the duration of our waiting we caught each other up about work. Liv gushes about the recent books she was sent, which are the same ones I was sent, by the recent authors we've worked with. We plan on picking one to read in December.

When it's Christmas, it's November. It's always November.

Suddenly, I'm in a trance, taken far away from here and back to wherever Declan is and brought back to the, what had he called it? The Kingdom of Flowers, back to when it was only me and him in that whole wide world, and I can't focus on the conversation anymore.

I'm rudely taken out of it by knocks on the door. Liv

releases a high pitched and quiet squeal. "It's him!" She takes a deep breath, many of them, before opening the door.

The door opens, presenting a familiar face.

There he stands with that same wavy hair that draped over his face when he stood over me, when we were lying in the grass. The face I was remembering in my mind only moments ago.

It's disorienting, seeing this face—this stranger's face that I saw months ago now—here, standing before me. Skin and bones. Existing before my eyes, before my friends. They both can see him and I'm not crazy.

Liv and Eren's banters are muffled. My head is light and trying to float away. The room dims until my vision is the size of a pinhole and the only thing in my plain of view is him.

He steps in and holds a hand out for me. "November? So good to finally meet you. I'm Declan."

I'd like to say that the next thing to happen was I graciously took his hand and we all had beers and talked and played some video games and had a good night, but I can't.

I don't know what they all did after I'd blacked out and dropped to the floor.

I CAN SMELL HIM. Even in the grass, under the clear blue sky, butterflies clouding the cold grassy knoll. He smells like a hundred scented candles. Sometimes books, sometimes pasta.

He sits against a tree, headphones on, eyes closed. It doesn't seem like he knows I'm here.

"Hey," I say, weakly. I prop myself up on my elbows and try to nudge his knee. My hand goes straight through him.

I get up and look around. This...bubble of ours...isn't empty like it usually is. It seems...normal.

Except for the woman that is walking toward Declan. That woman is me, but...not me. Her hair is shorter. Her clothes are nicer. Her walk is softer, lighter on her feet, which makes it look like she's floating. She kneels beside him. "What are you listening to?"

Without opening his eyes or removing his earbuds, or even without moving his lips, I hear him. *I'm listening to songs that remind me of you. Of us.*

"You silly man," she replies. She sits against the tree with him, her head leaning on his shoulder. She closes her eyes, too. "There is no us anymore. I'm gone, remember?"

No, you're not. You're still here. I can feel you, hear you. Sometimes I see you. You're not gone.

"It's okay to move on, my love."

But I love you. And I miss you.

"I love and miss you, too. But if you don't move on, you'll miss your chance at happiness. Your second chance at love is near. If you miss the opportunity, well, then you've missed it. I don't want you to be sad."

And I don't want you to leave me.

This is surreal. What the hell am I witnessing? I walk over and they can't sense that I'm standing right in front of them, watching this profoundly intimate moment.

They know each other. She's the me that he knew. She's the one he sees when he looks at me.

All at once, I understand. She's the November when it's Christmas.

CHAPTER 19

Declan

I NEEDED THAT. IT FELT LIKE HER. THOUGH SHE TRIED TO SAY goodbye, I couldn't, nor do I believe that that is the last time I'm ever going to see her. There's something in my gut that tells me that I'll see her again. In the meantime, I'll wait patiently.

Her presence flipped a switch in me and I'm coursed with a boost of energy. I work on chores I've been neglecting. There isn't too much dirty laundry but the clean clothes are in a pile on the couch. Nearly all of my dishes have been in the sink save for a plate, a fork, and a cup that I keep rewashing and reusing. Beer bottles are dispersed randomly around the house, including the back porch. Dirt I've dragged in has not been vacuumed for about two weeks. Countertops have not been wiped for days. I need to buckle down and make it look like this place hasn't been abandoned.

The first thing I do is break out my wicker basket of candles. I light one in each room of the house. I think of November as I do so, but this time, I think fondly of when I showed her my candle collection instead of turning into a sad, mopey puddle of tears.

In a few hours I've gotten the house back in shape. I'd even made myself my specialty pasta. I put on an episode of H3 Podcast, actually paying attention to it this time as I have not been lately, as I eat. Halfway through my meal I receive a text from Dean. He wants to discuss something with Karina and I, but not before letting loose and having some fun at an arcade with some beers. Anyone is welcome. Anyone's friends or significant others.

When I ask what this is all about he tells me that it's nothing bad and possibly exciting.

Karina asks if they are going to meet my mystery woman that I plan on bringing to the ballet. I think about it. After all, I did lead them to believe that I moved on, in a way. However, I can't bring Mia along with me tonight. November's got a chokehold on me. So I informed Karina, minus the chokehold part.

I find my mind wandering from November to wondering what Dean could possibly be wanting to meet for and talk about at an arcade and, if I'm being honest with myself, it's a nice little relief from the weight of November on my thoughts twenty-four/seven.

He said it isn't anything bad, which is good. It's got something to do with Karina and me, so it's got to be related to work. What could be exciting news for work, though? I desperately want to pester him about it but decide against it.

When finally we meet up at the arcade we grab our tokens and go crazy on the games. The last time I had genuine fun was when I took November for that boat ride dinner months ago. Tonight, I'm having fun. I'm loose. I'm free of heartache and grief. After a few goes on the basketball hoop Dean dares me to challenge Olivia to basketball connect four because he swears that nobody can beat her and he is right. She beat my ass twice and beat Karina and her boyfriend once each. I challenge Dean and Karina's boyfriend to the punching bag and Karina's boyfriend comes in first, Dean hits second hardest, and I come in just a few points shy from Dean's score.

The bumper cars are humbling, even for me, being the youngest in this group, but for some reason the impacts of the crashes are too harsh for our bodies, and yet, we are such barbarians that it could almost look like death is the goal.

Like the barbarians they are , they line up for another go on the bumper cars except for me and Dean. We tell them we're going to save a booth at the bar for when they're done. Dean and I get our beers and take a seat.

"Declan, man, I'm so happy to see you having fun tonight. I mean, I'm still so sorry about everything you've been going through. I can't imagine. November was a super sweet young lady."

My attention shifts to my beer because suddenly it's so interesting to look at.

"She was nice and Karina and I wished we could have known her better, but I'm glad to see you laughing and goofing around. It's, uh, certainly been a while since we've seen that."

"Thanks. "It's been a nice time. Thanks for the invite. And thanks for paying for all the beers I'm about to have."

"Oh, you wish, buddy."

We laugh and clink our bottles.

"Yeah, I apologize for my—"

Dean is already shaking his head for me to not finish my sentence. "No. You have nothing to apologize for, my friend. You have every right to feel everything you felt and deal with it how you needed to."

"No, Dean. Let me get this out. I know I've been moody and although I know that you guys understand where it comes from, I know better than to take it out on you and Karina. I wanted to take it out on someone and you guys were the unfortunate ones to be most available to me to do that. And my parents, my poor sweet parents, they caught some heat, too."

"Oh no."

"Oh yes. They would always ask how I was doing and if I was okay. Obviously I wasn't okay and it didn't help that they kept asking. But they did keep asking because of how miserable I looked. I would only answer their calls because they'd get mad at me when I wouldn't. So I'd tell them to quit calling because the conversations by that point kept leading to the same arguments."

"Well, in all honesty, you did absolutely need to talk with somebody, anybody, and if it counts for anything, I think it was good that your mother was on your ass about answering her calls. I think she knew, just like Karina and I knew, that if you needed to take it out on someone, that you could take it out on us. Release is release and we were willing to take the hits. We only wanted you to be okay."

"Thanks, man. I really do appreciate that." He pats my shoulder and we sit in short silence. "Anyway, what's going on? What are we doing here? Is this a work meeting or what?"

"Yeah, I guess you could call it that. It's more of a proposal."

I stare, waiting for him to say more.

"We'll wait for Karina. She's got to be here."

"Dean, you're making me nervous."

"No, no, no. No need to be nervous. It's nothing to be nervous about. Be...excited."

"Well go get her, then! The suspense is killing me!" He shakes his head no, so I get up and go to the bumper cars. They are in line again for a third round. I gently pull her out and everyone protests but nobody saves her. "Don't worry, I'll bring her back. Blame Dean." She pretends to fight me on it. "You want to know what we're here to talk about, don't you? Let's go find out and then you can continue to try to break your neck after."

Karina gets herself a beer and a refill for Dean and me and now we are ready to hear what he has to say.

"As you know, the three of us have worked so well together. Karina, you really know how to get creative and know ways to creatively solve our problems. Declan, you truly can make anything look and feel like dreamy art. And me, I'm good at planning and organizing and meeting with people and negotiating. We're a good team, wouldn't you say?" Karina and I agree. "How would you guys feel about switching things up a bit? I want to know how you guys feel about adding personal projects to our plate. Short films."

He waits for our first initial thoughts and reactions. Karina and I look at each other, I suppose to get a sense of each other's reactions as well. My brows draw together while hers is drawn upward. "Wow, I'm honestly surprised by this. What made you want to venture out to film?" I ask.

He shakes his head as he seems to be replaying the sequence of events that led him here. "I don't know. I was watching YouTube a few weeks ago and somehow got lost in the realm of short films. Before I knew it, I was having Olivia watch them with me. Then I noticed the lighting, background, angles, and story structure. The behind the scenes was also sort of motivational to be more creative. Learn more. Try something different. I'm not saying we'll be anywhere near full blown Hollywood production, not that I want that. I love the art and the craft of creating short films. Also, I'd love to see if we could enter our projects into statewide film fests and whatever else we could enter them in."

I can imagine both mine and Karina's brows shoot up at the thought of showing people something we would be complete beginners at.

"We don't need to go that far. We don't have experience with this stuff—seeking talent, writing scripts, directing, I know. And maybe eventually we can get there if we all want to continue but I've just been becoming obsessed with the idea of doing this, so I was curious if you might want to join in on this brand new journey." We're quiet, still processing. "It would be a very big commitment as I'm sure you can imagine. Time and money. So we could all have to be one hundred percent in it, heart and mind. But! Think of all the knowledge we'd be gaining. The new skills we'd be working on. The experiences this will bring us, the new people we could be meeting, the networking! Our imaginations would open up and go further in letting the impossible possible than we ever could in photography. Doesn't that sound fun and exciting? Come on, think about it. Really think about it."

Karina speaks first. "I mean, that does sound pretty awesome and fun. I'm just trying to think about the commitment part. It sounds like a lot."

"I'll be honest with you. It most absolutely will be a lot, but you don't have to agree to do this. It's just that you and Declan were the first people to come to mind when I thought about pursuing this. So if you think you can't commit or won't have your heart fully in it, don't be a part of this. It'll be a quick way to create friction within the project and then we'd probably bring that friction to work."

Karina taps a finger on her cheek. "Hm. Declan? What say you?" Her quoting of Aragorn was not lost on me.

Hm. What say I? I say that a long commitment to learning a whole new craft sounds like a good way to get my mind off of thinking about November and my guilt and my loneliness. What say I? I say... "I'm in." Dean bursts out with happiness at his first partner on board. We shake on it and just like that, I'm ready to put my imagined movies on a real screen.

CHAPTER 20

November

WHAT A FIRST IMPRESSION. COULDN'T I HAVE JUST PASSED AWAY from my embarrassment instead of having to wake up remembering what happened? I was mortified to have been informed that I passed out right after finally meeting Eren's friend, face to face. A face I know and recognize from across parallel universes. Declan, the man who has wooed me with beautiful words, soft gazes, gentle touches, and a kiss that was filled with pure longing. Declan, a man who I have come to crave to see and understand. So close after all, and yet still so far out of my reach. Now, with Liv in the mix, even less so. Dare I even say impossible.

Liv is video chatting with me to make sure I'm okay and keep me company. I wish she wasn't, though, because she won't shut up about Declan. *My* Declan.

"I told you he has the prettiest eyes, didn't I? And the greatest head of hair. He may not be a biker boy anymore but he looks like a movie star. He needs to be on movie screens."

The only response she gets from me are head nods. That's all I can manage to give because it's better than accidentally blurting that he's already mine. He's already chosen me. We've already sealed promises of the heart to each other, in some way, with that kiss.

"Hello? Earth to Em. Tell me what you thought about him."

My stomach churns and I inhale air and prepare to put on my best performance. "He's a looker for sure. He seems like the perfect little fling. A short-lived little fling." There. I said my peace.

Liv covers her face modestly, as if she is such a person. The squeal that comes out of her is not a sound I'm used to her making, and then I can feel what she's going to say next. "I can't believe I'm saying this, but I don't want it to be a fling. I'm not sure he wants it to be a fling either."

"But you guys just met. Has he told you that?"

"No, but it was a vibe. I was getting that sort of vibe from him all week."

"How?"

"Uh, I don't know. He said he really likes me." I stare blankly back at her so as not to give away my true emotions. She shrugs. "That's it? That's all you have to say about this, that he's a looker? Nothing about how I'm interested in seeing where things could go with him? Nothing about how he would be so lucky to date me—your best friend? Nothing about anything at all?"

I suppose I need to say something supportive. "Sorry. I think I'm just cranky from feeling sick all the damn time lately. So what does this mean, then? Are you and Declan a thing now or what?"

"I'm not sure. That's what I'm hoping for. I don't know him, so at the very least I would like to get to know him better. We're still texting with each other but not obsessively. I think we're both trying to play it cool."

"That sounds nice and all, it really does, but let's not cross off the men in this area. A relationship with someone in town would be a lot easier, don't you think? All I'm saying is be careful not to make things unnecessarily complicated." I hope I sound convincingly caring enough but I've had it with this conversation.

She gazes at me menacingly. "You know what? You're not telling me what I want to hear. Call me back when you're better because your sickness is not making you the most supportive friend right now."

"Ugh, you're right. I'm sorry again. If you want to pursue a relationship with him," I really don't want to give her my blessing, not that she's looking to have it or needs to have it, "then he would definitely be lucky to have you." But she's my best friend. *The* best friend. I need to be *the* best friend to her. Even if it hurts me.

"Now that's what I want to hear. See? That wasn't so hard, was it? It was like pulling teeth, but thank you. Now, what about you and Eren? How have things been with him? It's been months now. How much longer are you going to keep him on a leash? Or, I'm sorry, he wishes you had him on a leash," she laughs. "How much longer are you going to string him along? Have you been thinking about actually committing to the poor guy?"

"Why? Has he said something to you?"

"What? No. I'm just curious, especially now that I've got commitment on the mind."

"Well yeah, I don't doubt he's having fun with this arrangement but can't you see that he wants more with you? He's waiting to have more with you. He's waiting *for you*. And before you ask me if he and I have talked about this, no, we haven't. I'm just not blind."

"I'm not thinking about what he's waiting for, I'm thinking about what keeps me sane."

"Sane from what exactly?"

"Sane from—" I'd almost given my craziness away. Now I don't know what to say. "I don't know. The idea of commitment? The idea of what my future could look like? I don't know. All I know is that I love where I'm at right now. Is that so wrong?"

"Then maybe you can re-clear things with Eren. I feel like enough time has gone by and you should probably let him know where you stand at this point."

She isn't wrong.

He's excited to see me unexpectedly at his door and the first thing he thinks to say is to ask if this is a booty call. I know this isn't a relationship but the wooing doesn't have to be thrown out the window. I'm sure to keep my expressions in check. "Eren. Ever the charmer. I stopped by for a quick little chat."

"Are you sure you don't mean quickie?" he jokes, but I don't laugh. "Sorry. Come in." I take a seat on the sofa. He offers a beverage and I decline. "So what's up, Em?"

I begin to wonder when exactly did I become Em instead of November. I suppose he picked it up from Liv but I can't recall when even she started calling me that. Declan says my whole name and it's been making me want to go by November. Not Em. "Sorry I didn't give you a heads up but—"

"That's alright. You can just give me head."

I shut my eyes with exasperation by his constant dirty mind. It's starting to be a bit much. And maybe it's just the fact that I keep comparing him to Declan, which absolutely isn't fair. Eren is Eren and I like who he is. It used to be funny but maybe not funny anymore, knowing how he feels about me, though he hasn't expressed any true feelings to me himself. But Liv is right. He isn't seeing anyone else for a reason.

"What's wrong? I was only kidding."

"No, it's not you. It's—"

"Oh don't even finish that thought. 'It's not you, it's me.' Is that why you're here? It's the jokes, isn't it? I could tone it down."

Oh, boy. His eagerness for correction is going to make this hard. "Eren, stop. There is nothing wrong. I just want to sort of, I don't know, touch base with you about our casual relationship."

"We're friends with benefits."

"Yes."

"What about it?"

I didn't think about how I was going to word this, how to address this. I take a moment to think and he never takes his eyes off me and it's making me nervous and fumbling words even in my head. *Just be forward. Get to the point.* "I am still wanting to keep our relationship as that. Friends with benefits. What about you?"

Finally, his eyes wander thoughtfully. "Yeah, of course. I still want this. Why are you asking?"

"I want to make sure you know that if you ever find someone you want to pursue I won't feel bad if you want to end this. I'll understand."

He opens his mouth to say something but nothing comes.

"As long as it's not me," I clarify.

He rubs his hands together, smirking. "Hypothetically, if I want to pursue a real relationship with you, what would you think of that?"

I sigh. "I don't want a relationship."

"With me?"

"With anyone. At least not right now. I'm enjoying the quiet time I spend on my work, I'm enjoying not having any expectations to be a good girlfriend, and I'm enjoying you being in and out when we get together."

"Oh I enjoy being in and out of you, too."

"Eren!" I cry, not giving him the satisfaction of letting him know that that was a good one.

"Okay, okay. That's it. I'm done. Sorry."

I squint at him. "Man, I remember when you used to be quiet and mysterious."

He smiles. "When we've seen each other naked so many times and done the dirtiest things we've done to each other, mystery sort of goes out the window, don't you think?"

I remember, gleefully, the things he's referring to. He's got a point.

We sit in silence, waiting for the giddiness of our memories to subside. Then he breaks the silence to ask what I think of his friend.

Here we go again. "He seems nice."

When I don't say anything more, he replies, "Yeah, I love that guy. We've gone to the same schools since elementary but we didn't start hanging out until our first year of middle school. We couldn't be more different outwardly, but we're the same inside, if that makes sense. We found that out when we were partnered together for a project. We had to meet after school everyday for a week and we realized how much fun we had together. We've been inseparable ever since."

"That's beautiful," I say with slight sarcasm. "You guys sound like me and Liv." Since I didn't get the chance to get to know Declan, I wonder if this Declan is anything like the distant one, if they could be identical in personality, or exactly the same, or completely different. Eren says that they're different, and that's true with my distant neighbor. "It's a shame I missed the opportunity to talk with him. What's he like?"

"He's a softy. He's got a big heart. A lot of the boys in school thought it was cool to act tough and unafraid, whereas Declan wasn't afraid to show people that there's nothing wrong with a gentler edge."

"What about you?"

"I acted tough only when I needed to, you know? I was like him in that way, where we didn't feel the need to one up everybody all the time, but if someone wanted to act tough with me, I wasn't one to back down. If someone wanted to act tough with Declan, he was always able to walk away from the situation with a new friend. His scrawny quirkiness gave him that advantage."

"What's he like with women?" If my question was too forward, he hadn't let on.

"Oh, he's good with the ladies. Neither of us had any trouble there."

"Does he date a lot?"

He thinks about it. "I mean, he goes on dates but," Eren

looks as if he's discovering something about his friend. "You know what? He hasn't had many girlfriends. Mainly dates. Yeah, he dates."

"Ah. So he's a serial dater. Or a careful lover." My face reddens. That was meant to be an inside thought.

The remark does not go over Eren's head. His eyes squint and brows draw together. "Why? You have a crush on him or something?"

I give my best fake laughter. "No, you silly goose. My best friend is quite fond of him, though. Did you forget? All your complaining about them and whatnot?"

His shoulders slump with relief very subtly. "Right. Don't worry, your friend is in good hands."

"Is she? He sounds like he gets along real well with the ladies. Do you know how he feels about her?"

"I don't know. I haven't really asked."

"Why not?"

He stands. "Why are you grilling me?" he chuckles nervously. "Look, tell Liv that she's just going to have to ask him herself because I have no clue. I just thought they were having a good time. I didn't know how serious she was getting."

Suddenly, I'm embarrassed. I've been here long enough. "Sure, I'll let her know." I absolutely don't plan on telling her about this conversation. I need to stay out of this before I mess things up between them. "I better get going. Thanks for talking with me." I turn to leave but he takes my wrist and slowly pulls me into him.

"Hey. That's really all you stopped by for? To let me know that I'm released from this arrangement if I find someone I like? Or were you trying to find out if there is anyone I might like more than you?"

My heart skips from his intense stare. I know what he's doing. He's trying to keep my focus on his eyes so that I don't notice how close he's pulling me into him. He does that a lot but I catch on to it quickly. "No," I whisper. He lifts my chin. "I mean, yes. I mean, I just don't want to hurt you."

His large hand grazes my face as it makes its way to grip the back of my head. "What, you think I'm going to fall in love with you or something?"

I can feel the warmth of his breath. I can smell the toothpaste from his tongue. "No," is all I can think to say.

He puts his mouth to my ear, his hot breath going down my neck. "Good. I can assure you," he licks and nips at my ear, "that I'm not," his lips press around my neck, "falling for you," until his lips work their way to my cheek. "I'm definitely," he kisses my other cheek, "not in love with you." He plants his lips on my lips, his tongue creating an opening and gently colliding with mine. He sits on the sofa and smoothly pulls me on him. My legs spread over his lap, sitting on him, and his hands roam all over my back and my ass.

I can't keep myself from him any longer. His lust is always so excessive and fierce and needy. I throw my head back with a moan, inviting him to kiss my neck, my chest, my breasts. My hips move with greediness and impatience. I hover over him so that he can whip himself out. Once he's free I wrap my legs around him and pull my underwear to the side, inviting him in some more. Once he's in, he lifts me up with the force of his pelvis, pushing into me over and over as I grind on him.

In the moment, I wonder how I can be so caught up on Declan when Eren feels so damn good. I want to want Eren the way he wants me. It would make perfect sense. I wish I knew why I can't. When I try to convince myself to just jump in and go for it to see where it goes, I'm always compelled not to, by some force that's keeping me from doing it, sometimes to the point of dizziness if I thought too much or too hard about it.

Eren gets up with him still in me and carries me to his bed. He places me gently on his soft cotton comforter and lays me down, never pulling out of me, and begins pounding in me like his life depends on it. His whimpers make me rub against him faster and harder. He's going to finish soon and I want to finish with him.

I moan so loud I surprise myself and yet, when we finish together, my brain wants the final thing I see to be Declan.

Declan in the grass.

Declan in the flowers.

Just Declan.

CHAPTER 21

Declan

I STAND AT THE MIRROR LONGER THAN NECESSARY. FIRST, I TIED MY tie too tight, then I loosened it too much. Now, it's tight again and it's making it hard to breathe. I decided against wearing a suit altogether and changed into a softer pair of slacks and a dark navy pullover knit sweater. I have no clue what people wear to ballets anyway, so this is a better choice. I'll neither be too dressy nor too casual, but a perfect in-between.

My phone rings, previewing a photo of Mom and Dad on their wedding day. I answer. "Perfect timing. I just finished getting ready."

"Merry Christmas Eve!" they say together. "Sweetie, let me see your outfit. I want to see the suit," Mom demands.

I turn my camera view around to face my full length mirror. "I changed my mind about the suit. This is more comfortable. And I don't want to be overdressed, too, you know?"

"Oh, Deccy. I really wanted to see you in that fancy suit," she sighs disappointedly. She tilts her head. "Oh, you know what? That looks really nice, Deccy. Yeah, I like this look, too. What do you think, Hun?"

Dad says, "Son, you look sharp. I think I like this more than a suit. The suit was too much."

"Thanks, guys. This will be my first ballet. I'm kind of excited. I never thought I'd be excited for a ballet," I grin.

Mom and Dad eye each other and then back at me. Mom says, "Or you're excited to go on this date." She smirks.

"I've already told you that this is not a date. No one else is going to this alone, and I didn't want to be the only one going solo, so I asked a new friend. No big deal."

Dad asks with a raised brow, "Does your new friend—"

"Her name's Mia," Mom chimes.

"Right. Does your Mia friend know this isn't a date?"

I'm five seconds too long to answer because I really can't remember how I asked it. "She knows that it's not a date."

"You don't sound too sure, Deccy," Dad replies.

Once again, I take too long to respond and Mom cries out in mock horror. "Oh! Deccy, how could you?!"

Dad closes his eyes, probably anticipating a rant from Mom when we get off video chat.

"Mom, it's okay. I'll talk with her on the way. She'll be okay, I promise."

"Oh, Deccy. Okay. Just be nice to the girl and don't make

her sad. But I wanted to ask, is there any chance that you might date her in the future? Could this, uh, friendship sort of be headed in that direction at some point?"

I wipe a hand across my face and grunt out a deep breath. "Mom, I don't know. I just want to have a good time with my friends tonight, that's all. I have to go now. I'll call you guys later, okay? Love you. Bye." I hang up even though Mom tries to frantically get the last word in.

On the way to pick Mia up from her house I think about Mom's question, about if I might date Mia sometime down the road. I try hard to imagine what we could look like as a couple. I can't.

I ring her doorbell and she opens it in seconds. "Mia," I say, frozen. "You look...great. Festive." She has on a long shiny green dress. It's very simple-looking, and not. It seems like she is also going for an in-between look. Her blonde hair drapes over her shoulders in big curls. Her makeup is expertly done with a smoky red on her eyes and a dark red on her lips.

"Thank you. You don't look too bad yourself." She throws on a dark brown coat and takes my arm as we walk to my car. The moment we step off the porch she stops dead in her tracks.

"What is it?" I ask.

"Do you see that?" She gasps. "Do you feel that?"

I don't see or feel anything.

She looks up and smiles. "It's snowing," she says softly.

Now I can see the flurries underneath the streetlights.

"Oh, yeah. Hopefully it keeps up and then we can finally have another white Christmas."

"Yeah, that would be nice." She closes her eyes, enjoying the small flakes falling around her. "Okay, we can go now."

When we take off for the ballet we get to talking about Christmas plans. "My plan is to video chat with my parents as we open gifts. I'm excited for them to open their gifts from me. I got Mom an upgraded treadmill that inclines, as she's very much into her health as she's gotten older. I got Dad a new golf set. His current one is a secondhand set from one of his buddies years ago. I also got them a couples gift. A gift card for the movie theater. They love going out for movies together."

"Wow, sounds like you went all out for them," Mia says, impressed. "What do you think they got you?"

"Candles."

She laughs, unimpressed. "Candles? Really? Do you even like candles?"

I think about the time I showed November my candle collection. "Yeah, I do," I admit through a stifled laugh.

Her face softens. "Oh. That's very sweet, then. May you get more candles this Christmas," she says cheerfully.

"What about you? What are your Christmas plans? What did you get for your family?"

"Unlce Robert and I are going to drive to my parents' house tomorrow. I got my mom a Coach purse and a set of Coach earrings. I got my dad some camping gear. He's been talking about wanting to go camping next year, so I got him a few things to get that going. And for Uncle Robert, I found an artist to paint a portrait of him and Aunt Helena. And it's framed."

"Really? That's incredibly thoughtful. I know he'll love it."

We sit in silence for a little while and then she says, "So... you like candles, huh? I nod. "I didn't mean to—I only laughed because I thought it was such a parent-y gift. I love candles. I love that you love candles."

I chuckle. "It's okay. I get it. What can I say, I like a nice scent. It's nice to have them on hand."

She nods.

"What do you think they got for you?"

"Candles."

"Shut up," I blurt. "For real? Candles?"

She cringes and laughs. "Candles."

"CAN you believe it's really snowing?" Karina asks as Mia and I walk toward the group waiting outside the theatre entrance. "Hi! I'm Karina! This is my boyfriend, James. That's Dean and his wife Olivia. And you're Declan's mystery date!"

Before Karina can say another word, I say, "Yes, I told you I was bringing my new friend. This is Mia." Mia and

Karina look at me when I refer to her as my friend. "She is my neighbor's niece."

Mia shakes Karina's hand and Dean and Olivia steal her attention, to which Karina takes the opportunity to lecture me. "Friend? I thought you said—"

"No, you assumed. All I said was that I had asked someone to join me."

"Yeah, and you couldn't correct me? I almost referred to her as your girlfriend. In front of her! Ugh, that would have been so awkward."

I shrug.

"Ugh. Sometimes I forget how young you are."

I shrug again.

"So the two of you are only friends? No romance in the future?"

"Who knows?" I put an arm around her and guide her to everyone else. "Come on. Let's go watch some ballet, huh?"

Our seats are pretty good. They are at the very back row, dead center to the stage. Not bad at all for free tickets. Mia sits to the right of me, Karina on my left. Dean and his wife are in front of Karina and James. I never knew this place existed. The vibe is fantastic, electric with sophistication. Huge. The stage is much bigger than I imagined. This is no school play production, this is the real deal.

"Thanks so much again for inviting me to this. I love these types of things, especially around Christmastime. It's my absolute favorite."

"Yeah, no problem. There was no way I was going to be

the only one showing up alone, you know? It's good to have you here."

"So no girlfriend? Girl*friends*?"

I look at my hands and twiddle my thumbs. I'm not sure if I want to tell her about November or not. We're here to experience a wonderful show and I don't want to bring the mood down, but I also want to be honest. I breathe in, preparing to keep this brief and quick, to rip the bandaid off. "I was in love—" I bring my head up...and see that the whole theatre is suddenly empty. I turn my head...and see her. " —with you," I finish.

She watches me with patience. *Go on*, her big soft eyes demand. *Keep talking.*

I don't question how she is here. There seems to be no point. Neither of us have answers. I believe this is just the way it's going to be. I shift in my seat to better face her. "I was in love with you, still in love with you. You're gone and yet you still come to see me. You said I need to move on, well, here I am, trying to, and yet..."

She plays with a part of her shirt, quietly contemplating something. I don't interrupt. "You—" she put her hands flat on her lap, eyes meeting mine. "You said that you'd love me in every world."

I study her face, trying to read her, waiting for more.

"Is that true?"

My eyes soften. "Well, you are November Nolan, aren't you?"

"Yes."

"Then yes." I gingerly pull her hand to my lips and kiss her soft skin. I close my eyes, soaking in the moment.

She slightly wiggles her fingers and her eyes turn sad.

"What is it?"

"Our time is up."

No. I shut my eyes and hug her whole arm. "No."

She pulls her arm back and runs a hand through my hair and down my face. "It'll be okay." She grins with confidence. "I'll see you when it rains."

Rain? Not in my case, but... "I'll meet you in the flowers."

CHAPTER 22

November

I WILL. I'LL MEET YOU IN THE FLOWERS.

The face that now sits beside me slowly turns and points forward. "Watch the show, creep." Dad is rarely ever serious, especially towards something like watching grown men in leotards jumping and dancing, but he seems to be really into it. I admit I might have been staring at him like a creep, but a moment ago it wasn't him that I was looking at. I wasn't looking *at* Dad. I was looking somewhere...beyond.

Mom and Dad are here to visit for Christmas Eve because they are going to spend Christmas day with Mom's family. Her three sisters, one brother, and one of Dad's brothers.

They arrived a couple days ago. Liv came with me to pick them up from the airport and they met Eren, my special friend as they keep calling him, yesterday and they'd been trying to encourage me to date him. Of course it doesn't help that Eren keeps trying to sweet talk them and woo me in their presence. Needless to say, my parents love him. I wish I could love him the way they all want me to.

I missed my chance of meeting *my* Declan and Liv met him first. Had I just been there instead of staying at home to see the other one I'd have him for real and not in the rain, not in the flowers, not in my dreams, and not in my fantasies. I often wonder if I had been there to meet him the same time Liv did if he and I would have hit it off instead. I imagine yes. I imagine I would have walked into that bar, laid my eyes on him, and become hypnotized. Liv would have noticed my attraction and given me space to do my thing and cheer me on from the sidelines.

This is my fault.

He misses her, the me that exists in his world, and the universe is giving me to him, handing me over on a silver platter and I don't even have a say. That's what I believe. He'd said he'd love her in any existence. Well, here I am, existing all the way over here. It could be possible that we are meant for each other in every existence.

And that's the way it'll be.

The next time I see him is March in the new year. I stopped going to his house and started running to the flowers, where he said to meet. I waited against the tree he leaned against when the love of his life was trying to say goodbye for good and tell him to move on. It was astonishing and scary and miraculous all at the same time to see a parallel version of myself. She was more...flowery. Softer. I'm harder. I've become a wall to shield myself from another bad relationship.

My mind drifts in this eerily familiar place almost forgetting why I'm here when his voice reminds me. "Hey, neighbor."

I sit up from the wildflowers, remembering exactly why he calls me that. "Hey, neighbor," I say back. "It's been a while, huh?"

He sits in front of me, knees up with his arms around them. "You remembered."

I nod.

Without changing his sweet demeanor he shyly looks down and says, "You know...I–I know that...you're not...her." He looks back up at me with a tight lopsided grin.

It's my turn to look down shyly because we both know it, and I got lost in him—his love, his pain, his grief, his longing—and I played the part. "I'm sorry."

He let his smile grow and a chuckle released. "Don't be. It's my fault. But can I ask...why did you just...let it happen?"

I shrug. "It seemed like you needed me to be her."

My words strike him but he goes on like it doesn't. "We were supposed to be each other's forever, and how can I deny you when I keep seeing you? I know it's selfish and wrong and weird—Am I wrong for this?"

I genuinely don't know how to answer that. "Am I wrong for wanting it?"

"No offense but how can you even say that? You don't even know me."

"I know you loved her, *how* you loved her." I search deep in his eyes and wonder if we both want to live how we want to in this bubble that is our own, or if we want to bring reason and reality into it and let it burst. I search as deep as I can for an answer. All I see is that he is giving me that choice. So I choose us. "I want that."

I choose us.

"Hey, neighbor," he has started saying on a regular basis. It's because of the way I signed the very first letter I wrote him. It's cute.

We are lying in the grass watching the clouds drift by when he asks how it feels when I'm suddenly transported here. He says that he hears a loud cracking sound, similar to when lightning strikes something, then all sound abandons him, though not lately. Lately, it's been changing. Almost like everyone and all activity around him simply whisks away.

I tell him that it started out the same way for me. "Lately, I can feel it as it's about to happen. My body becomes weightless yet my feet are still planted on the ground. The noise of my world shuts off. I see white. I can no longer tell if it's lightning or just my vision as I enter this parallel universe. And it's always raining."

"I love rainy weather."

She scoffs. "Why does everyone say that? It's just rain. So what?"

"What is your beef with rainy weather?"

"When there's rainfall, I fall. Let me explain. I'll fall into a state of panic. I'll fall into a state of anxiety. I'll fall into a state of dread. I mentally prepare myself for something unfortunate to take place. All my young life I've associated such depressing weather with tragedy. The tragedy of having witnessed a car wreck where a young life was taken. The misfortune of having to bury my pet rabbit in the rain because it lasted for days and my poor little Sugar's body could no longer stay above ground. The horror of getting caught in the rain with classmates at school and a boy slipped as he ran for cover and bashed his face on the concrete. I watched his blood pool in the rapidly growing puddles. I had never seen so much blood before then. It scared me.

"Then of course, watching my mother grow sicker and sicker from what she told me was a thing called pneumonia and explained to me how she caught it. She only had it for a few days but she went through a terrible time. I vowed never to catch that sickness.

"Well into middle school I had grown anxiety around rainy weather. And for those reasons, I could never understand the coziness of a stormy day."

"Do you still hate it? Even now?"

I know exactly how he means it. "No. Now I love the rain. It's how I see you."

His mouth curls slightly upward. "I was hoping you'd say that."

"HEY, NEIGHBOR." He has a couple of filled champagne flutes and I clutch my chest, feigning esteem. He sits in the wildflowers with me and hands me a glass. "To...whatever this is that allows us to see each other."

"To seeing you in the rain."

A corner of his mouth lifts. "To meeting you in the flowers."

We clink our glasses and down the drinks in one go.

"You're around more and it makes me mad." He looks pained or panicked and I immediately interject. "Where I'm from, you're around a lot more now. You're with my best friend. Liv is amazing and everything, but...it was supposed to be me." I hang my head down, embarrassed to have said that out loud.

Silence hangs in the fresh air. We could have either been waiting for my disappearing act to come or imagining the thing I'd just said.

"I wonder if you had ended up with me if...this" he gestures all around us, "whole situation would still be happening or not." He blinks, thinking. "If not, I'd never see her face again."

My body slumps.

"Oh no. I've said a wrong thing, haven't I?"

"You don't want me, not there." I bury my face in my hands. When I feel his hand smooth my hair I lift my head and see his face nearing mine for a kiss as I was departing.

"My neighbor is a monster. She's always on my ass about showing off my body, mowing my lawn, watering my garden, making out in my front yard—" I'd messed up. There's been this unspoken pact that we don't talk about our personal relationships in our worlds, unless that's just me. However, at the mention of making out with someone, Declan deterred his focus from me to pulling out strands of grass. "Sorry. I wasn't—"

"No, it's okay," he smiles tightly. "It would be delusional of me to think that you're not being chased after."

I blink at him as he continues to fuss with the grass. "If only it was you that was chasing after me."

He looks at me then. He shakes his head in thought, brows furrowed and eyes wandering. "I must not be very bright, huh? How could I see you and not feel the way I did when I first saw you?"

"I was too late. And when we did meet for the first time, I fainted. My first impression here, I'm sure, was better than that mess."

"Still."

"No. You're you, just not to me."

"That can't be."

"It is. At least it seems to be. Every time I see you and my best friend together I feel you. And when you look at me, I'm a stranger. And it hurts." He takes my hands in his and squeezes them tight, not saying anything because he knows nothing will help this impossible situation. "Oh my god, I'm sorry. I didn't mean to bring this conversation to its grave. I was talking about—"

"Helena."

The hairs on my body stand. "How do you know my—"

"I guessed. My neighbor's late wife's name is Helana."

"Helena's dead?" I ask sadly.

He purses his lips realizing that now he is the one killing the light conversation. And then his eyes light up. "Ask to try her cookie recipe."

"Congratulations! That's huge!" I pat his back and lightly push him at the shoulder over and over with pride and excitement.

"Thank you, thank you. It was amazing."

"Wait, how come you never told me you were working on a short film?"

He winces. "I wasn't sure it was going to go anywhere. I wasn't sure how getting into all this was going to unfold. I honestly thought that we'd all get sick of the extra time together or get too burnt out, but turns out we really like this creative process. It's been fun. And it's been a while since we last spoke. A lot's happened."

Time was going by so quickly. His hair changed. It's shorter and the curls have all been cut away. It looks good but the transformation hit me like whiplash. I lay my head on my knees and admire his new look. "You can say that again."

"Dean wanted each of us to write down a story idea that we could work with and we'll have random people in our lives vote on one. Guess who's story got chosen. Go on, guess."

"Hmm...yours."

He nods, wearing a bright smile that I'm going to dream of tonight. "Mine." He stops nodding but his eyes stay glued to mine. "Now, guess what my story idea was."

Slowly, I lift my head, feeling something serious from his tone despite the smile on his face. I take a deep breath and really think about it. My lips part wanting to guess the story about us but I don't want to seem vain.

Though I say nothing he begins to nod again, as if he knew what I was thinking.

My head tilts, I squint as if it could help me to read his thoughts. Was I reading them right?

"Us," he whispers, as if he were telling me a secret.

"You and her."

He shakes his head. "Me and *you*."

I MAKE sure to be the one to say it first this time. "Hey, neighbor!"

He runs to me without a word and a smile on his lips. He holds me tight and kisses me delicately and desperately.

After I catch my breath I say, "I missed you, too."

"HEY, NEIGHBOR," he greets first with glee. As he walks to me I am sure he notices the dark circles around my eyes.

I smile anyway, wanting him to ignore them. "Hey, you," I greet back. I go in for a hug and he stops me by the shoulders and stares, hard. I keep my head down but he isn't having it. He ducks low enough to meet my gaze. "Can you stop?"

"November, what happened?"

"You should see the other guy," I joke. He doesn't find that funny.

He stares deep in my eyes instead of around them, waiting for me to explain the dark circles.

"I...haven't been sleeping well. That's all."

"Okay. Why? What's going on?"

"Life!" I shout. I turn away from him and throw myself

into the tall grass. He takes his usual place in front of me. I choke out, "It's hard for me over there."

He rubs my legs. "What's hard, November? Tell me."

I open my mouth to tell him but stop myself. Instead, I say, "Why? What's the point? What help can you give to me when you're here and I'm there? What help can you give to me when it seems like we're waiting longer and longer in-between before we meet again, even though it feels as if we're getting to have more and more time here from when this started? What use is that?"

He sighs, no doubt from his own feelings about it. "We're here now. Tell me."

I stand up and talk behind him, not wanting him to watch me so intently as I bare my dreary feelings. "I'm losing my mind. I can't handle seeing you with my best friend. Each day you guys are getting closer and closer. Each day I pray that something terrible will get in between the two of you. Each time I'm with Eren I feel guilt because he cares so much for me and I picture you every time. No offense, Declan, but sometimes I wish that I could just be in love with Eren. He's there for me, all this time. If we could choose who we get to love, my world would not be filled with hate, hurt, resentment. My self-esteem would be higher, I'd be kinder, my mind stronger, maybe I'd feel fulfilled, and my heart would have joy. I would choose Eren and you would move on. Or I would choose you and Liv would choose not to love him."

I wipe my tears with my shirt. "If we wake up now and

smell the dead roses and see the world for what it is, a flawed world filled with hurt people, then maybe we could wake up and smell the roses that have just blossomed and only see the good things around us, but if you're walking with blinders on you're bound to walk into a thornbush. Maybe I'm the thornbush, Declan. Maybe you need to turn away from me. I'm hurting everyone around me."

I hear him get up from the grass. "If it makes you feel any better, I'm going through the same thing."

"It doesn't," I snap, wondering if he means that he's also with someone for physical affection.

He walks in my plain of view, frustrated. "Okay, I'm sorry, but don't go around saying stuff like...like...I'm not even sure what you're trying to say but I don't like the way it sounds. What are you trying to say? About choosing who we love and...and...and you being a thornbush and...and...how I need to turn away from you? What is all that, November?" He sounds out of breath.

His hands are on his hips. I notice a ring on his finger. I think I just died inside. I stare at the ring as I ask, "Is that why you feel guilty? For me? Or for her?"

He doesn't even have to look at the ring to know that I'm staring at it, but he looks like he got caught doing something wrong. But he isn't in the wrong, of course. This situation is what's wrong.

"No."

"No what?"

"*No* I don't want to talk about this," he holds up his

finger with the ring. "I don't want to waste any more time. Come on." He lays in the flowers and pats the space beside him. "Let's have a nice time before it's up."

I get on the ground and lay my head on his chest, tears silently spilling out of my face. I soak in this wonderful scene. The sky is burning the clouds with hues of neon pink, purple, and orange

Here I am with the love of my life, the one I'm meant to have, supposed to have, in this bubble of space and time that is made just for us and I'm going to ruin it. "I don't want to exist."

I can't see his face, but I can imagine he closes his eyes with pain or wanting to block that out. "Don't say that," he simply says, rubbing my shoulder.

I hand him a folded paper.

He freezes before taking it. "Wow, we haven't written in a couple years."

Without looking at him, I say, "If I could stop coming here, I would."

I hurt him. "Come on. Don't say that."

I'm nothing but a thornbush and, "I don't want to exist anywhere."

part three

CHAPTER 23

Declan

"Declan?" Mia asks from behind me.

I'm slowly coming back to reality. I'm outside at my car. I was supposed to be getting something. I don't know how long I've been standing out here like this.

She put a hand on my shoulder and it's helping to bring me back from wherever she thinks my mind goes when I'm "gone". That's how we started referring to my momentary leave of conscious absence. After two years, she still knows nothing about how I leave to see my one true love.

"Yes, dear?" I ask drowsily. I've returned but I wasn't ready to go. What the hell did November mean she doesn't want to exist anywhere? I worry that she'll go and do something that can't be reversed and then I truly would never see November ever again.

"Can we please call someone about your blackouts? They're really starting to scare me."

I don't turn around as my eyes are glossed over with pain, but I groggily say, "Just go back inside. It's passing. I'll be in soon."

I can feel her hesitation from concern but eventually she says, "Alright. Take your time." She takes the box of diapers that I now recall that I was supposed to get. "Also, your daughter is ready for a bedtime story from daddy." Mia plants a kiss on my cheek and goes inside our house.

Our. House.

At the mention of my little girl, the haze of my daydream clears up. *My daughter. I need to get to my daughter.*

I read the note first.

Declan,

I apologize if I seem out of sorts. I've slowly been filling up with resentment. My attitude spread to my best friend and we weren't talking for a while. Sorry to mention him, but Eren tried to help mend our friendship and I pretty much tore his head off. He stopped talking to me. I failed my deadlines for work and Liv couldn't ignore that. She threatened to demolish our business—my dream business—and our partnership. In the midst of a heated argument she called me jealous. Of her and Declan. Of her and you. That hurt because it was true.

While you're not him, he is you and it hurts whenever I see the two of you together. And I hated myself—always hated myself—whenever I let my jealousy get in the way. At one drunken point before I managed to get everyone to hate me, I'm pretty sure I had told you and Liv that it should have been me. Eren didn't find that funny at all.

I made a mess over here. I'd like to say it wasn't all my fault, that these pains come from somewhere, but it's my fault for spreading my pain. I took it out on everyone. I no longer know who I am. I don't know how to be a functioning person anymore. I can barely get out of bed. I don't know how to exist knowing that the only person I care to spend the rest of my life with is not even in the same universe as me.

While I was trying to be who I should be for these people who give a shit about me I am losing my fucking mind at the same time. How is it fair that I have to be what they want me to be but I can't express my anger for what it's done to me? Why do I have to fight my anger? Why do I have to watch you build a life with my best friend? Why do we live so close and yet I have to wait for the storm to see you? Whose bright idea was it to disguise this curse as a blessing?

It was a cruel joke to ever have met you, Declan. I love you and I can't be with you. I'm sorry. This is not your fault but I am stuck with seeing you. And you're stuck seeing me whether or not we want to.

What am I to do, Declan? Tell me what the hell is there for me to do.

When the tears are dripping, spilling, falling without the gasps, without the fight to breathe normal, without the shuddering and the shaking, without the panting and the holding yourself...when you're just...frozen but the tears are escaping like they are people jumping out of a burning building, desperate for relief...when that's where you're at, you must have had to go real far to disconnect from yourself. Me, I'm so far gone I'm not even in my own dimension!

Again, I'm sorry.

Until next time, neighbor.

I close the car door, reminiscent of my first meeting with the other November flashing in my mind, and I make my way to my daughter, ripping up the letter and putting it in the garbage can on the way.

I'm reading to my baby girl but the pictures look like a love story of me and November.

When she falls asleep, I go into bed, kissing my wife goodnight, but I only see myself kissing November lying in the grass.

I fall asleep but my dreams are movies of myself and November—*my* November—falling in love as we did from the very beginning as I sit in an empty theater smiling at the plot. The scene changes to my life with Mia and suddenly the theater is filled with other movie-goers. They say *Awww* to the part of our first date. They cry happy tears with Mia as she informs me that she's pregnant. The scene changes again, to the other November and the theater is empty again. In the movie, she's crying. She's sitting at a dinner table with her best friend and an imposter of myself. Her best friend and the imposter are eating spaghetti the way lovers do and November is just sitting there crying to be seen, but they can't see her or hear her. I stand from my seat and go to the large moving picture of her. I reach a hand up to touch hers. I pretend I'm holding it. "I'm right here, November."

And as if she hears my voice, she stops crying, but her eyes are empty and looking nowhere.

Lying in the flowers is different these days. My heart fills with contentment instead of longing and, if I want to be brutally honest with myself, I can feel that I am finally coming to peace with it. Slowly, but looming. This is still a kingdom of love, but for the love of my unexpected wife and our surprise child.

I didn't plan this life. I wasn't going to choose this life. Yet, against my own judgement and wishes, it still chose me. And after a while of Mia and I dating, I could hear November's voice clear as day. *It's okay to move on, my love. If you don't move on you'll miss your chance at happiness. Your second chance at love is near. I don't want you to be sad.*

I've been thinking a lot about the last time I saw the other November. No matter how much I love her she'll be hurting because of me. I know that it should have been extremely obvious that there's nothing I can do to fix anything for her. She's not real, not in my world. You can't save someone that's not real.

What's real is the effort that Mia puts into our partnership and it hasn't been fair that half my heart has been somewhere else, with someone else. What's real is my little girl and lying here with her in the kingdom. With butterflies. In the flowers. Not a thornbush to be seen.

"Aww, look at my two loves," Mia says as she walks over with a picnic basket.

I sit up and say, "Oh, look. We made mommy carry all this by herself. That's what happens when little girls," I say as I boop her tiny nose, "drag their daddy out of the house because they're too impatient." I get up and dust myself off. "Here, let me help you." I lay the blanket out and plop my little princess of the kingdom on it.

Mia gets herself settled on the blanket and unwraps an egg salad sandwich to feed it to the princess. "Alright. What have I missed?"

I unwrap one for myself as I say, "Well, we saw a heart cloud, a giant dragon cloud, and little miss princess here said she saw a fart cloud. And then she kept repeating the word fart and laughing for three straight minutes." Mia has a good laugh at that. "And then a butterfly landed on her hand and we just watched it." I can't help but wonder if it was my November, or a sign that she was watching me build a life, a real and happy life, without her and that she's happy for me, for all of us.

Or if the butterfly was just a butterfly.

Also in the basket are some toys. The little princess takes out the bottle of bubbles and kindly demands it be opened. As soon as I open it she takes it and runs, or wobbles.

The sun is hitting Mia's face just right. She's golden and

glowing. Her pale skin already a light red from the walk over here. She lays her arms on her knees, resting her chin on her arms. I watch her watch our daughter with adoration. I watch her with adoration.

I'm caught staring. "What is it?" she asks with a smile.

"What is what?"

She searches my face for something. I don't know what. "For as long as I've known you, you always seem to have something on your mind. I want to know what it is, right now. You're just...staring at me," she laughs shyly, like we haven't been married for nearly two years, "so I want to know."

I take my time as I get on all fours and crawl my way to her. I invade her space with my body until she's lying flat on the blanket. Her eyes fill with delightful curiosity and hunger, not for a sandwich. "You're beautiful," I say. And though a glimpse of when November and I bumped into each other at the bookstore trespassed my thoughts, I couldn't not say it. Mia is beautiful, inside and out. "You're such a good wife. You're such a wonderful mother. I was only wondering," I inhale a deep breath, "how I got so lucky."

The hunger in her eyes turn tender. "Oh, Declan." She put her arms around my neck. "I'm the lucky one. You're amazing. You won a film fest award, you're now working in the film industry, you're a great provider, and a wonderful father. I know we didn't plan for a baby, but I'm happy about our...little accident," she cringes at the phrase. "I just hope you never feel like I—"

"Don't even think about finishing that thought." She was going to say trapped. I'll admit that in the beginning I did feel trapped, but I never once believed that she intended to trap me. She used to cry about it all the time because she believed that that's how I felt. She wasn't too far off, but it was agreed that we would try to make it work. She was all in while I was half gone. The guilt ate me up. The guilt of not being fully with her, and not being fully with the other November, and from moving on from my November. My guilt came from all directions and I felt like I didn't deserve a life with Mia. I regret this but at one point I gave up in hopes that she would be the one to make the hard decision to leave. That wasn't fair and it certainly wasn't right.

"Don't say it, ever." I lightly trace her face with the tip of my finger. "I want you to know that I'm here for us. I want to be here for us, the three of us, and I will be."

Her brows draw together. "I know that."

"I love you, Mia."

"I love you, too, Declan."

I give her gentle kisses all over her face. "You're my world." *My real world.* "You and our little princess, Ember."

CHAPTER 24

November

Wait. Wait…no. The rain pouring off my lashes makes it hard for me to see ahead even though I know I wouldn't see Declan, but I wasn't ready to leave. Being ripped away from him was so damn frustrating.

"November!" Liv shouts through the noisy rain from the dryness of the back sliding door. I ignore her.

Eren is beside her. I hear him tell her, "Her blackouts have grown longer than before, but I've learned that she doesn't like it when you try to take her out of it."

"I know but look at her," Liv replies.

Take me back. Take me back.

Nothing.

"Take me back," I say, though not too loudly. "Take me back. Take me back," I keep repeating.

I feel Liv's hand on my shoulder. "Okay, let's go back inside."

I rip my shoulder out of her tender grip and shout into the angry night sky. "Take me back!" I cry. "I'm not done yet! Take me back!"

I imagine the scene freaks out both Liv and Eren because in the next instant they get in my way to bring me into the house. I try to shove them aside because they don't know what they're keeping me from, or that they were keeping me from something.

Eren squeezes my legs and hauls me over his shoulder. All my physical energy dispels but I continue to cry out.

Liv closes the sliding door behind us as Eren sits me down at the kitchen table. Declan goes around me and covers me with a towel. I can only stare into his eyes, hoping that he would remember that in a different world, he loves *me*. His eyes avert mine and pain pierces through my chest. My spilling tears make it feel as if I'm still getting rained on. "What are you guys doing here?" I ask, bothered.

Liv takes the seat in front of me while Eren and Declan stand behind her. Liv explains, "I texted you earlier that we were coming over but you never responded. I assumed you would have seen it at some point." When I don't respond, she continues. "But I mean it's a good thing we did come. You were...having one of your blackouts in the rain. You're normally scared about getting sick. Getting struck by lightning. Like, what were you even doing out there?"

I don't feel like trying to yet again come up with why I've been doing the things that I've been doing over these last few years. "Liv."

"Yeah?"

"Could you please make me some tea?" I just need her off my ass for a bit. All of them.

"Of course."

While Liv is making my hot beverage I think Declan is suddenly aware of how close he is to this weirdo. In my peripheral vision, I see that he signals to Eren to follow him to the other room. They don't know that just because the rain is slamming down hard all around the house that it doesn't mean that I can't hear the echoes of their voices in the enclosement of the house.

"So I've been wanting to ask you this for a long time but...the entire time I've known her, she's been off. Weird. Selfish. Rude. I tried to be friends with her, especially for Liv, but I just can't and I don't get it."

Eren's deep voice booms through the silence within the house. "You don't get what?"

"Why you think you love her."

My heart wants to shrivel up and kill me right here.

"Shut the fuck up," Eren replies.

"I didn't mean to—"

"Shut the fuck up," Eren says again. "You don't know her."

"I mean, she treats you like—"

"Don't you fucking worry about the way she treats me, alright buddy?" I hear a slap to his shoulder, I assume, and probably a slap too hard.

"You don't deserve—"

"I'm a grown ass man, Dec. I don't need you to tell me what I deserve. I love you, man, but as I said, shut the fuck up."

"Okay, but tell me *something*. Her obsession, or hatred, with rain is odd. She looks at me weird, like she either loves me or wants to skin me alive. You guys came here for an intervention or something. Is that still going to happen?"

Intervention?

"She's been going through something. Her blackouts started around the time you first met them and Liv and I don't know much about that. Liv really wanted us to talk with her about her attitude toward all of us, not just you. She and Em have been...at odds with each other for a while now and Liv is past the point of anger and has entered a stage of worry. And if Liv is worried, then maybe we should get to the bottom of it to see if we can help her." Eren sighs. "I miss who she was. She was cute in front of people, hot in the bedroom, proud of her job, talented, and we could talk about everything and nothing. It was so comfortable and easy with her. I'm willing to fight with her to get her back not just for me, but even for Liv, and for herself as well. I wouldn't be able to live with myself if who she was goes to waste. She needs our help. That's all. And she sure as hell doesn't need your judgement."

Eren. Sweet Eren, my knight in shining armour.

Liv gives me my tea and goes to the other room to tell them both that although she can't hear the entire conversation, I probably can and for the both of them to shut the fuck up.

They speak in hushed tones and I can't make out anything they're saying. I sip on my steaming hot tea and it warms my insides, which helps to relax my muscles. My heart is no longer racing and the heated and sad feelings I had with the other Declan a few minutes ago have subsided, and I try to remember what even happened in our little glimpse of time and space before I vanished before his eyes for the X amount of time. I lost count. This has been going on for years now and I wish it to stop.

The three of them are back in the dining room with me. Declan puts on his jacket and Eren comes to my side. He kisses me on the cheek. "We're going to head out, okay? I'll come by tomorrow morning. Declan and I will bring you girls some yummy breakfast."

I feel nauseous, appalled by my behavior. He's so sweet to me, after all these years, all this time, and through all of my mistreatment toward him. I'm too ashamed to respond. Without looking at him, I nod.

The men leave and now it's just me and my best friend. At least, I hope she's still my best friend.

"I told them to leave," she says. "I'm going to spend the night with you. Keep you safe. Keep you well." She embraces my head to her chest. "What were you doing out there?"

With total emptiness, I reply, "Enjoying the rain."

I don't fight her on taking me for a weekend getaway, especially so that we can rebuild our friendship. How could I? She's willing to fight for what we had before I ruined everything. Before I started being weird around her boyfriend, before I kept trying to give her boyfriend signs that I could be interested, before she lectured me about treating Eren unfairly just because we were never official and I accused her of being jealous that there's a man so desperate for me, and before she called me jealous for wanting Declan.

Before I started giving both her and Eren the cold shoulder. Before Eren tried to move on from me but kept coming back to check on me and ruined it with the girl he was seeing, short as that fling was.

We've never gone through a rough patch before, not in any way that truly mattered, and I had really been testing the boundaries with my unusual and foolish behavior. The fact that she came back around to work on this with me—or work on me, let's be honest—is a true testament to who she is as a friend. I don't want to let her down.

Maybe I won't. The forecast calls for perfect weather for the foreseeable future. We settled in our shared hotel room. We are within walking distance from everything we could possibly want and need. Book shopping, clothes shopping, restaurants, and bars. Our retail therapy retreat is something that could help bring me back to normalcy. All I need to do is be present and, well, be her best friend.

As we unpack I pull out a bottle of champagne from my luggage. “Surprise,” I say, smiling.

Liv is pleasantly shocked. “Em, you party animal” she exaggerates. “Yes. Let’s.”

I untwist the wire of the bottle, cover the top with a kitchen towel, and tug at the cork until it pops, thankfully without spillage. I pour a coffee cup for each of us. “I want to toast to you...for not giving up on me despite the way I’ve been acting over the last four years.”

“Girl, I’ll toast to that.” She holds up her cup to clink mine but I’m not finished.

“You’ve schemed with Eren to make sure that I was being looked after behind my back even though we were in the state of hating each other.” Liv waves the conversation away but I’m compelled to keep singing her praises. “I know that you told Eren what my comfort foods are so he could make them for me on the nights he stayed with me. You still loved me through your growing distaste in who I had become. I had animosity toward you because...because...” *Oh shit, am I really going to tell her?* “Because Declan is who I see when I have my, as you guys call it, blackouts.”

Liv’s eyes lock on mine, unblinking and unmoving. Slowly, her brows draw together as her eyes squint, trying to see honesty or a lie in me.

Bringing her serious boyfriend into the conversation, especially when he’s the reason I caused our issues, may not have been the best idea, but maybe it's about time she knows why I've been the way that I've been, and towards her boyfriend, no less. "I know it sounds crazy, like the way my stroked-out story from years ago sounded but I swear to you that this is why—"

"Wait," she cuts me off. "Are you...seriously claiming... that..." she closes her eyes and puts a hand to her temple as she knows she's about to suggest something impossible. "You've been seeing Declan, someone we had never met prior to the night of your delusion, while having blackouts? November, tell me how the fuck that's possible and why you expect me to believe it. Please. Because you are about to ruin this whole..." she gestures all around her and gives up on finishing the thought. She doesn't need to.

"I don't expect you to believe the situation but I suppose I was hoping you would believe me. I know it's hard. I know how impossible this sounds but I knew his face before we ever met him, yes. That's what I'm saying. And then... because it kept happening, I...started to grow feelings for him, hence my animosity about your relationship. But that's no excuse for treating everyone so oddly and I'm sorry. Liv, I'm so sorry." I desperately want to tell her our theory, my and the other Declan's theory, about how we were meant to meet that night and fall in love, but of course I'm not about to push my luck with her.

She releases a heavy breath and her shoulders slump. "Let's *pretend* that what you're telling me is true. I'm still the one seeing Declan. *Dating* him. And you didn't respect that, which means you weren't respecting me. That's fucked up."

It's my turn to release a breath and slump my shoulders. "I know. I'm very sorry about that. I know what reality is now. I need to live in reality. I understand that now."

"Do you really think you're in love with Declan?"

"No." How could I? The version of him I fell for loved me first. That's all.

"Remind me again why you don't want to be in a relationship with Eren." I can tell that she is holding back a tone she really wants to use. "He's adored you since he first met you, he agreed to be your friend with benefits for a long time, and he's never left your side even though I warned him that I thought you were into his friend instead."

"It wouldn't have been an honest relationship. Would you have preferred I fake my intentions?"

"No, it just never made sense to me. He's cool, he's hot, he's sweet, and he's devoted to you. I don't know why you wouldn't at least give it a shot."

I shrug. "Perhaps I will, now that the fog in my mind seems to be clearing up. Now that it is, I don't know what I was thinking all this time, with you...with Declan." I lie back on my twin bed and put a pillow over my face, pining for suffocation.

Liv comes to my bed and sits on my hips. She takes the pillow off my face. "It's okay. This is what this trip is for, so we can go back to normal. It's a reset."

I selfishly think about the other Declan and his wedding

ring and how he's never told me about her—about his real life. Anything could be happening. He could have been hooking up with so many women until he found a new, real love. He could have several kids by now and I never knew. He's moved on and my heart stayed with him. He's moved on and I'm just a ghost of his former love that blinks in and out of his existence. I don't mean anything to him in the grand scheme of things. A tear spills out and slides down the side of my face. "I don't know how I can recover from this."

Liv purses her lips with a contrite smirk. "Don't worry, Em. We'll get you there. And we think we know how."

We?

CHAPTER 25

Declan

"HAPPY ANNIVERSARY," I SAY TO MIA AS I PUT HER BRAND NEW sparkling diamond necklace around her neck. I kiss her cheek and take my seat across from her.

She breathed, "Oh, Declan, this is way too much."

I'm more than happy with her reaction. "Is it really? Because your smile is telling me otherwise." The reactions of the other restaurant guests also seem to be impressed."

"Well, I mean, I'm not going to tell you to take it back. I mean, come on. It's mine now, you just should have re-thunk it before getting it for me."

I take her hand from across the table. "No. You deserve it. You've been so patient with my new career path. You are my number one supporter in my transition into filmmaking with Dean and Karina. You literally have helped make this transition to be so smooth and not as stressful as I thought it was going to be. Mia, you've been the best wife and the best mother to Ember. I wish I could give you more than this silly necklace tonight."

"No, stop with that. You know what you give to me *and* Ember. Please, we don't need to be stroking each other's egos right now. What you *can* do is order this chocolate cake for us."

I order the cake and another refill of red wine for Mia.

"Are you trying to get me drunk?" she jokes.

"Absolutely not. I want you to remember everything we do tonight at the hotel." I down the rest of my beer as our eyes lock.

"Can't wait," she says with a devilish grin. "I need to go to the ladies' room. I'll be right back." She scoots out of her seat and excuses herself.

I watch her body move in her sexy little red dress. She's always had great style. She looks incredible in everything. She could make a potato sack look sensual. I'm really lucky to have taken my chance with her, rocky as it began. I'm lucky to have had November's voice in my head, and her blessing to move on. I'm glad I didn't pass on Mia because of the guilt I bore at the time.

I thank November in my head. I thank the November that released me from her love, not the one that was destroying her real life because she had to have me. So much time has gone on without seeing her and I wonder from time to time if she's okay, and almost as if I manifested it, beyond the seat of my wife's chair, I catch a glimpse of November crying in her bed, writhing in pain.

My heart races and I rub my clammy hands together. I'm still in the restaurant, everyone still in it, yet here is November right before my eyes. I can see her. I can hear her. I wonder, if I reach out, could I touch her? Would she feel me?

Would it matter?

All at once, she stops crying and sits up as if someone has walked in on her.

Me?

She turns her attention in my direction. I don't know if she can see me or if she is looking at someone I don't have a view of but it seems like she's looking straight at me, then pops something in her mouth followed by a sip of water.

And just like that, she's gone and Mia is back at my side trying to wake me from a false blackout.

"There you are. Are you okay?"

"Yeah."

"Come on. Let's get out of here." She put her purse on her shoulder and takes my hand to help me up.

"Wait, the bill. The cake."

She shows me the little foam box. "I had them pack it, and I paid the bill already."

"Oh, uh, okay. Yeah, we can get out of here."

I have gotten used to not seeing November anymore but now, I can't help but hope that she will be okay.

November, if you can hear me, feel me, sense me, know that I want you to be okay.

All I want is for you to be okay.

CHAPTER 26

November

LYING ON THE SAND FEELS DIFFERENT THAN LYING IN THE FLOWERS with Declan, who I haven't had a single glimpse of in nearly a year. In my early stages of, let's say running with my delusions, I could barely imagine life without being transported into his world and seeing him.

Now, things have been different since my parents, my best friend, and Eren have all decided that being on depressive medication would be good for me. Of course I had to undergo a few sessions with a therapist, who agreed that I sounded severely depressed. The only thing she really had to go off of was that I was in love with my best friend's boyfriend, and her conclusion was that watching them fall in love over time was breaking me.

No shit.

Three sessions later she concocted a magic potion in the

form of a pill that will transform my gloomy skies, the skies that tell me Declan is near, into colorful art meant to inspire positivity.

Since being on meds I have tried to start another beneficial relationship as friends with Eren, and I knew he wanted it, but he kept denying me. I kept trying, though, because a girl's got needs, and what this girl doesn't need is to go out into the dating world meeting strangers. I'd prefer the comfort of my own...Eren.

We're looking up at the twinkling stars when I say, "Thanks for this nighttime beach trip. It doesn't feel like you're trying to get in my pants at all."

He laughs. "I'm not."

"Why?"

He doesn't say anything.

I turn on my side to face him, propped on an elbow and resting my head in my hand. "I've told you before, the meds have been working. I've been good. I've changed. Haven't I changed?"

He blinks up at the sky, surely contemplating on if he wants to say what was on his mind or keep it to himself. Or at least keep it from me.

"Is there someone else?"

"No."

"Then..."

Eren sits up. I dust the sand off his back and sit on my legs. He's quiet for what feels like a long time but I'm willing to wait as long as it takes for him to give me something.

He let out a long breath. "Something just...never made sense to me. I don't know if I should bring it up."

My body tenses with eagerness. "Yes. Ask me anything. I'll be honest. If it'll help us get back to before, I'll answer any question to the best of my ability." This doesn't surprise me but it makes me nervous.

"Okay. So...what I would like to know is..." I know the question he doesn't want to ask. "Why are you in love with my best friend? I mean, I get it, he's an amazing guy but you barely knew him before, and even now."

I knew this was coming eventually and everytime I'd pretend to answer, I could never come up with what I would say. But here goes nothing. "I think there was a mistake in my heart when it said love at first sight. Something romantic radiated from him. Something soft, sweet, and... poetic."

"You're not wrong. He's all of that. So what now? What, uh, what is there for you to do with that confirmation?" I appreciate that he doesn't ask this spitefully but rather curiously.

"There's nothing to do. I had a moment of acting on instinct just because they were right when really I didn't have to act on it at all. My brain and heart wires had gotten crossed and well, it seems now it's all fixed."

He stares into the darkness of the ocean. I let him process. I want to lay him back and rest my head on his muscled chest as his strong arms embrace me but I refrain.

"So...you like your men...poetic?" he asks awkwardly with a half grin.

I put my face in my hands. "Oh shut up. Please." I hear Clare de Lune play on his phone. I put my hands down and he is standing over me holding a hand out. I take it and he gently pulls me up into him. We sway to the music. The light sounds of the small waves crashing and splashing makes the moment feel magical, like I'm living in a painting.

He gazes into my eyes, commanding my attention in a different way than I'm used to. "November."

He rarely says my whole name. It was a pleasant surprise to hear it slide out between his luscious lips.

"You're beautiful in the way Clare de Lune is beautiful. Your heart is soft and filled with romance. I didn't see that about you before. I looked for what I wanted to see in you and forgot to see your heart. I'm sorry. I messed up."

Messed up? That baffles me. "What? No. You didn't mess anything up. I'm the one who messed up. I'm the one who is sorry. I'm sorry, Eren, for everything. I'm sorry for keeping you an arm's length away. I'm sorry for being the reason why your other relationship didn't work out. I'm sorry for wanting you for selfish reasons. And I'm sorry for thinking I was in love with your closest friend. I'm sure there's more to be sorry for and I am, I'm sorry for those things, too." My forehead rests on his chest. I close my eyes wishing that none of this ever happened.

He must have felt my shame. He puts a finger under my

chin and lifts my head so I can face him. "Hey, it's okay. I mean, we were never dating. It's okay. I'm okay."

"You deserve a good woman."

"You're a good woman."

"You deserve better than me."

"Would you say that I deserve to get what I want?"

"Yes. You deserve what you want and so much more. You're such a good fucking guy. You're...perfect."

"Am I perfect for you?"

I'm not prepared for this conversation that's sounding very...commital. "You're perfect," I say again.

"For you?" he repeats as well.

"W-What is this? What is happening right now?"

"November."

He says it again. Is this the spell I needed to break my curse? This song? This dance? His poeticism? My name off his lips?

"The next time we fuck," and there he is, "I want it to be as an exclusive couple."

I stop dancing. "Really? But why? I don't understand what's so great about me. You could literally have any woman you want."

"You know the way that you described how you felt, or thought you felt, toward Declan? That you couldn't help it?" I nod. "That's how it is with you, how it always was with you. I'm pulled to you. *You* pull me in. I can't help it. In my mind and heart, I feel like the universe wants us to be together, *needs* us to be together. I don't know, I just want you. I only want you."

My eyes go big. I want to laugh at the thought of him feeling like the universe wants us to be together while I was feeling like the universe wanted me to be with Declan. My legs move me away from him, turning my back to him, as I ponder this notion. In the grand scheme of things, maybe the universe doesn't know what the fuck it's doing after all. Maybe *it's* broken. I turn back to him. "Are you...in love with me?"

"I mean, I don't know. I can't know until we, you know, date first. Feel us out. All that good stuff."

I smile at this hot, sexy, sweet, soft, and romantic man. He's got to be it. He's got to be the real deal.

"November," he says with his hands buried in his pockets and shoulders raised, "be my girlfriend. I've waited years for you. I don't want to wait anymore. We're only getting older. Be my girlfriend. Let us finally build a life together."

I try real hard to picture a life with him. I don't know what's different now where I can see it, a happy life with him, but I can see it. I can see us happy together. I put my arms around him. "Okay, okay. Quit begging." I kiss him hard. I had been needing his lips on mine for a long time. If this is what it takes, fine. Declan is done and now I need air in my lungs. Now that this whole thing is over, I feel like I can breathe better.

Could just be the meds, though.

He tries to pull me back down to the sand but I have something else in mind. I take off my shirt, which stuns him. I slip my sweatpants down to my ankles and step out of them. He's seen me naked before—many times before—but his eyes inspect me like he's never seen this much of me, in a bra and undies.

I reach a hand to my back, teasing to unclasp my bra. I get a smile out of him. A shy smile, as he must be seeing me in a new light, as his woman, finally. And then...

My bra loosens but I keep it against my chest.

"What are you doing?" he asks, out of breath, grinning.

"This is all water under the bridge, right?" He nods. "Well...let's go skinny dipping in it." I pull my bra off and at the sight of my bare chest, he comes running toward me and throws me over his shoulder and runs to the water. I scream, thinking that he's going to drop me in it without letting my body slowly adjust to the temperature but when he puts me down, the water is only ankle deep. "Uh uh," I say. I pull his shirt off and undo his pants and tell him that this is a no pants zone.

He looks around. "Someone might see us. Those, at least," he gestures to my bare breasts.

"I think we'll be okay for a little while. Come on. Chop chop. Your girlfriend requests it."

He throws his pants as far as he can and pulls me further into the water.

My breasts press into him, his big hands cup my butt. We make out like we're teens that snuck out to see each other. I've got to say that there is something incomparable about making out with him as his girlfriend versus as a friend with benefits. I desperately hope that this feeling will never go away. I'm done dreaming of far-off places and impossible romances.

CHAPTER 27

Declan

The princess of the kingdom has just come home with her mother. Mia gives me a kiss and prepares a bath for the two of them. While Ember waits for the bath I sit her at the table and we munch on cookies I just finished making—Mr. Thompson's late wife's cookie recipe that Mia has long since perfected and taught to me.

"How was the kingdom?"

In four-year-old speak, she says she had a nice time being with the butterflies. There's always butterflies there.

I stare at her—my daughter—in awe, in disbelief that I have a child. A four-year-old. And I'm a dad. And I'm married. After all that I thought my life would be after losing November, I still found love. As I watch Ember, I just can't fathom my life. Being in my thirties, I feel like life has finally begun.

I don't know why November doesn't show up anymore

but I hope she's doing better than the last time I glimpsed her. Sometimes I'd find myself wondering if that was about the Declan imposter or something else. That was the last time I saw her, on my anniversary last year. I wonder if all of that is in the past now.

Ember. You are my world. My everything. I will keep you safe from harm. I will give you all that I can. You'll grow up happy, your mother will teach you this cookie recipe, I'll teach you film production and photography and you can have a fun career in your future, and if not, you can be anything you want to be. Your mother and I will support whatever makes you happy. Life is about finding joy and that's all I ever want you to feel. You are my life now. It's your world and I just live in it. This is Ember's world. When it's New Year's day, it's Ember. When it's Easter, it's all for you, Ember. When it's summertime, it's Ember. When it's Christmas, it's Ember—my baby girl.

CHAPTER 28

November

My body has morphed into one that I barely recognize. My typical cardio and balanced eating habit is no longer doing anything for me and lately it's been making me feel insecure about my weight gain.

I must not have been paying attention when my doctor must have explained the side effects for my depressive medication because when I looked it up a few days ago the medication is indeed the reason for my steady weight gain.

Eren, my serious boyfriend for nearly two years now, is madly obsessed with my new body. I, however, feel like I can barely recognize it as my own. At first, I thought maybe it was just an aging thing, now that I'm well in my thirties. It's been a long time since I've seen Declan. This could all be over and I could get off my damn meds that's altering my body and distorting the way that I'm seeing myself.

Goodbye, medicine. You've done me well but from now on, it's time to do this on my own.

WE'RE RE-WATCHING POLDARK, the show we started when Eren first started laying thick hints about how he felt towards me. I'm lying on my side with my head on his lap. His fingers comb through my hair, a habit he's picked up over the years.

The gloom outside darkens the whole house and creates an atmosphere that makes it difficult to keep my eyes open. The distant rolling thunder helps lull me to sleep. I don't fight it for too long before I give into the pleasure of slumber as I listen to Poldark and Elizabeth squabble in a way that only true lovers do. Passionately. Painfully. Regretfully.

I listen as I recall the same feeling of not being with my one true love and being forced to watch him fall in love, harder and harder, with someone else. Those days are gone. Eren is my one in this world. He is the one that's chosen me again and again. And I choose him because he really is everything. It's been clear to me that even when the universe was forcing me to see someone else, it was false and a miscalculation. This, I would tell myself for any of it to make sense.

And then Eren pauses the TV, assuming he needs a bathroom or a snack break. Groggily, I ask, "Can you pop some popcorn while you're up, please? I need something to wake me up and nibble on." He doesn't answer. "Hey," I say, patting around me trying to find his leg or arm or anything. I don't feel him at all. I open my eyes and sit up. The TV is off and Eren is nowhere to be seen. "Eren?" My heart pounds fiercely, panic building as I am aware of the familiar atmosphere.

This used to be the part where I would run to him. Run to our Kingdom of Flowers.

Not this time. Not ever. I lie myself back down and close my eyes, waiting for this to be over.

CHAPTER 29

Declan

She didn't meet me at our meeting place months earlier, and now here I am again. I was going to walk to the kingdom but now, I think I'll go straight to the source.

I go next door. *Knock knock knock.*

There's no answer.

I knock again. I put my ear to the door and seconds later I hear quiet movement on the other side. Of course, it can only be one person. "Hey, neighbor." I swallow, readying myself for a speech I didn't prepare for but I need to say *something.* "I...don't see you anymore. Do you know why? Do you know what happened?"

More silence.

I sit against the door and wait as long as I can. I honestly waited for it to be over but it was seeming like it was going to be one of those long ones. "I've missed seeing you. A lot has happened in the last, what, seven years? I'm not sure anymore. I've lost track." I knock lightly. "November, are you there?"

Nothing.

"November, I...I waited for you. I just want you to know that. After all this time, I waited for you in the flowers." I cover my face with my hands, exasperated. Maybe there isn't anyone beyond the door. I turn the knob but it's locked. "If you're in there, know that I still care about you. I have a family now—I'm married to...an amazing woman and we have a daughter. It took a long time for me to move on from us, from whatever we ever were, and...I'm happy now. I hope you're happy, too."

I can swear I hear a heavy breath release through the door.

"You were never her...and you were never going to be her. You're you...and you were enough—*are* enough—in *your* world...for someone else. Eren. If even I can see it worlds away, please tell me you saw it, too. I hope you did and I hope he makes you happy."

I press my ear on the door again when I ask, "If we can't be lovers, November, can we be friends?"

CHAPTER 30

November

It feels as if my heart is pounding so hard in my chest that it's practically banging on the door. Old feelings want to resurface, but I breathe...and breathe...hoping they won't take over me the way they did before.

Why now? Why, after all this time, why—*My medication.* I stopped taking it. I want to crawl away and pop one in when—

"If we can't be lovers, November, can we be friends?"

I clutch my heart. This is too much. Too beautiful and too much. I take my time twisting the lock on the knob. When it clicks, I pull air into my lungs and slowly expel it through my mouth. I very hesitantly twist the doorknob. I'm so nervous to see his handsome face. Will it cast another spell on me and undo everything I have done to give myself fully to the best man I've ever known in my whole life? There's only one way to find out.

I open the door just a crack. I stand up and hear him get to his feet as well. Here goes nothing.

I open the door wider and here he is, lovely as ever, except his hair still cut short, no curly locks in his eyes. His smile lines are more visible. He's gained good weight. Those piercing eyes, though, are exactly the same. They look at me exactly the same way. "Hey, neighbor."

He spread his arms apart, his face asking if it's okay to give me a hug. I think about it momentarily before I decide it's okay.

When we embrace, it's friendly and warm. The lust is gone from the both of us. It's wonderful.

When we part, he asks, "So, uh, shall we take a walk to the kingdom? For old time's sake?"

I look beyond the clouds trying to feel an answer from the universe. I get nothing. "Uh, I think...I think I'm...done." My eyes fill with sorrow that I hope he can see.

His smile drops a little but immediately lifts back up. "Oh. Right. Yeah, I understand."

I see that he does understand my meaning exactly, hurt as he looks. We both feel the bittersweetness of needing this to end, and not just for me.

"Come on," I tell him. He watches as I lie myself flat on the grass of my lawn. I put my hands behind my head and wait for him to catch on.

He's by my side moments later, lying as I lie. "Do you know why?"

I laugh. It starts subtle and then bursts uncontrollably.

He laughs a little with me. "What? What's so funny?"

"I was taking antidepressants. I think that was why. I recently stopped taking it because I was gaining weight from it. I've been doing well, anyway, so I also figured I could live without it. Yet, here we are again."

He props himself on an elbow. "You do seem better. You are as beautiful as the first day I ever saw you, dripping rain and all."

I don't know if he's only being nice but in the moment, I find that for the first time, what he thinks doesn't matter as much as it used to. That's a good sign, one that I needed. "And you, a deer in the headlights."

"Hey, you can't blame me. Anyone would freeze up if someone appeared out of thin air."

"You're not wrong. I was terrified. I didn't know what was happening, where I went, where all the noise had gone."

"Ah yes, the dead quiet. I've had many near panic attacks because of it."

We are quiet for a long time, no doubt the both of us revisiting our own memories together in our own heads.

"I never congratulated you, so congratulations," I mutter.

"For what?"

"Your marriage, your child, your wonderful life."

After a minute of silence, he says, "Her name is Ember."

I turn my head to him. I know exactly who he's referring to, and why. "For her."

That must have struck his heart unexpectedly as his eyes water instantly. He looks back up at the sky. "For her," he agrees. Then I watch a tear slide down the side of his face.

I look back up at the clouds as well. "Even though I'm done here, I want you to know that you'll always have a friend across the galaxy."

"I hope you'll think of me when it rains."

"I hope you'll think of me...fondly."

"Always."

CHAPTER 31

Declan

I GUESS THAT'S THAT. SHE'LL BE BACK ON HER MEDICATION, leaving me—us—in her memories. I'll have the memories and the short film that will someday become a bigger production film.

That's it for us.

The curtains have closed.

The End.

CHAPTER 32

November

THE RAIN SOOTHES HIM UNLIKE THE WAY IT NEVER SOOTHED ME, back when I was at odds with the natural showers from the sky. I stick my hand out from the porch and catch the soft falling raindrops in my palm. I run my hand over his delicate head, slicking back a patch of his thin hair.

He stirs ever so slightly in my arms at the cool touch and I bring him back to the porch swing and rock him back into undisturbed slumber.

Eren comes out with two mugs and I cover up with a throw blanket before taking the warm cup in my hands. Only now, damn near forty, am I beginning to understand the coziness of the gloom, the chill, the taps of wet drops splattering all around me. No thunder, no lightning, just a bit of drizzle to put my baby boy to sleep.

Our boy, created from the embers of what my life was, a

dumpster fire, and after Eren, he built a cozy fire within me and we produced Ash.

My phone dings with a text. "Declan says that he and the kids are going to surprise Liv with a book of their own." I hold out my phone to show Eren the photo Declan sent.

"Oh yeah?" Is that what your best friend, Declan, is texting you?" He looks at the photo. "Oh wow. That's pretty awesome. Reply to him saying that I think it's super cool and that I remember a time when he and I were best friends. No offense, Em."

I roll my eyes. "You know, to be in the book industry for so long and she's going to be getting a special made photo book of their lives is such a thoughtful gift. She's going to love it. But that also reminds me, I also need to get her a birthday gift before her dinner."

"We want to go with you." He looks down at Ash. "Don't we, son? Yes, we do. We want to go shopping with mommy, and then daddy will get you stuff, too."

I pat the space beside me on the swing so that he can come back with my baby. "Yes, daddy will get you everything you want," I agree.

Eren boops his tiny little nose. "Anything. Sky's the limit."

Sky's the limit. I shake my head light enough that he can't see because little does he know...

It's not.

Epilogue

Dear universe, I thank you for my time on this earth. I thank you for the rare experience I got to have in another world. But I'm going to ask you for this favor one last time. I hope I'm not too late.

On this day, a familiar storm, I have prepared myself to visit an old long-distance friend.

I close my eyes and as I wait for the universe to take me and try to imagine a place I haven't been to in so long. His house, the street, the Kingdom of Flowers.

I concentrate on the tappings of the heavy drizzle on the window.

At first, I got glimpses of how I remember it, and then the longer I saw it in my mind...

"We've got to stop meeting like this."

One second I envisioned I was standing in the middle of the street, the next, I'm standing in overgrown, tall, wildflowers. "That was the—" I said as I turned and saw him, "—plan."

"I like the hair." He points to my short silvery bob.

I study his new face. It's different from the way he looks in my world. It catches me off guard. "Oh, Declan," I breathe, tears filling to the brim of my eyes. "What happened?"

Only half his face is smiling. "What? Oh, this?" He tries to move the side of his face, forcing it to smile. "Just a little stroke. It's permanently numb. The grandkids love it."

At the mention of grandkids, I think of his daughter, Ember. And I think of my own adult kid, Ash. I never even thought about the two of them together, their names fitting like a puzzle. Finally, my tears fall, dropping like heavy stones.

Declan walks to me, leaning on his cane for help. "My friend, please, please don't cry for me. This was nothing."

I don't listen to him. In fact, I instead fall to the ground and weep. "I'm sorry," I say into my hands.

He kneels beside me, slowly as his old bones allow. "My dear friend, what are you sorry for?"

Through gasps, I say, "S-So much time...too much time... wasted. I cut you out. I said I'd be your friend. Who does that to their friend?" I lie back in the overgrowth and cry into my hands.

He follows my lead. He let out a tired breath. It seems like so much to bring himself down with me. "*Time.* What a bastard Father Time is, huh? I know." He put his hands underneath his head. "November, tell me about your time. Catch your old friend up."

I clear my sobs and dry my face. "Where do I even begin?"

"What happened after we last spoke?"

I bring myself back in time to that emotional parting of ways that was my doing. "Eren and I were in a new relationship. We flourish with ease." I recall the memories of all the ways he'd taken care of me as I was stuck in gloom. He made sure I ate, made sure I worked, made sure I stayed entertained with drama shows, and most importantly, kept me up with my best friend when I wasn't speaking with her. "He's a good man. Good husband. Amazing father...and grandfather. We lived a beautiful life filled with so much love."

"How many kids do you and Eren have?"

"One. A boy, I mean, a fully grown man now. Ash."

"Ash," he repeats. And then laughs. And then laughs harder.

"What?"

"My daughter's name is Ember. Your son's name is Ash."

"Ah, yes, I caught that. What about you? Tell me about your life."

"Mia and I have four grown kids, two girls and two boys. We have five grandchildren. Our life was also filled with love."

As he speaks, I can feel a shift in my breathing. I knew what was coming. The rays of the sun are dimming.

"That's...amazing...to...hear." I try to speak with strength but I think he notices something is off because he turns to me with a grim expression. I was hoping I could leave this place before my final breath but I'm trying to hold on as long as I can.

He props himself on his side. I keep my eyes averted from him.

"Eren is...already gone. Ash and the grandkids...think I'm doing well. I don't want them to..."

"Shhh," he interrupts. "Save your breath, November."

My eyelids flutter. The clear blue sky is going dark.

"November, I want to say thank you for showing up in my life when you did. I know we'll never know how, but I'm grateful for your presence. You are not her," I know who he means, "but you are my most special friend."

My voice won't work. *You are special to me, too. You've always had a special place in my heart.*

"You were my miracle to make me believe in miracles."

You were mine, too.

"And you'll always be my distant neighbor."

I feel his lips press on my forehead. And something wet on my face. I can't tell if it's a fallen tear or a raindrop. At one point, they were practically the same things to me. I used everything I had left in me to say with my final breath, "Goodbye, neighbor."

underneath his head. "November, tell me about your time. Catch your old friend up."

I clear my sobs and dry my face. "Where do I even begin?"

"What happened after we last spoke?"

I bring myself back in time to that emotional parting of ways that was my doing. "Eren and I were in a new relationship. We flourish with ease." I recall the memories of all the ways he'd taken care of me as I was stuck in gloom. He made sure I ate, made sure I worked, made sure I stayed entertained with drama shows, and most importantly, kept me up with my best friend when I wasn't speaking with her. "He's a good man. Good husband. Amazing father...and grandfather. We lived a beautiful life filled with so much love."

"How many kids do you and Eren have?"

"One. A boy, I mean, a fully grown man now. Ash."

"Ash," he repeats. And then laughs. And then laughs harder.

"What?"

"My daughter's name is Ember. Your son's name is Ash."

"Ah, yes, I caught that. What about you? Tell me about your life."

"Mia and I have four grown kids, two girls and two boys. We have five grandchildren. Our life was also filled with love."

As he speaks, I can feel a shift in my breathing. I knew what was coming. The rays of the sun are dimming.

"That's...amazing...to...hear." I try to speak with strength but I think he notices something is off because he turns to me with a grim expression. I was hoping I could leave this place before my final breath but I'm trying to hold on as long as I can.

He props himself on his side. I keep my eyes averted from him.

"Eren is...already gone. Ash and the grandkids...think I'm doing well. I don't want them to..."

"Shhh," he interrupts. "Save your breath, November."

My eyelids flutter. The clear blue sky is going dark.

"November, I want to say thank you for showing up in my life when you did. I know we'll never know how, but I'm grateful for your presence. You are not her," I know who he means, "but you are my most special friend."

My voice won't work. *You are special to me, too. You've always had a special place in my heart.*

"You were my miracle to make me believe in miracles."

You were mine, too.

"And you'll always be my distant neighbor."

I feel his lips press on my forehead. And something wet on my face. I can't tell if it's a fallen tear or a raindrop. At one point, they were practically the same things to me. I used everything I had left in me to say with my final breath, "Goodbye, neighbor."

ALSO BY AMANDA SIMONS

Duende

In My Healing Era